HALFCOCKED

BOOK ONE

SAN DIEGO PARANORMAL POLICE DEPARTMENT

JOHN P. LOGSDON
JENN MITCHELL

D1520927

Published by: Crimson Myth Press (www.CrimsonMyth.com)

Thanks to TEAM ASS!
Advanced Story Squad

This team is my secret weapon. Their job is to help me keep things in check and also to make sure I'm not doing anything way off base in the various story locations!

(listed in alphabetical order by first name)

Audrey Cienki
Bennah Phelps
Carolyn Fielding
Cindy Deporter
Emma Porter
Hal Bass
Helen Day
Janine Corcoran
Julie Peckett
Karen Hollyhead
Kathleen Portig
Larry Diaz Tushman
Leslie Watts
Malcolm Robertson
Marcia Lynn Campbell
Mary Letton
Melony Power
Michelle Reopel
Myles Mary Cohen
Nat Fallon
Paige Guido

Penny Noble
Sandee Lloyd
Scott Reid
Sharon Harradine
Terri Adkisson

CHAPTER 1

Jin

A bullet in the head beats two in the chest.

— JIN KANNON

*P*rojectiles cracked the wall he was facing. From his count, there were seven gunmen.

It wouldn't be enough.

He sat on the ground, waiting. His guns were holstered, his hat was tipped forward, and his arms were crossed. There was no point in doing much more than resting, so he took advantage of the opportunity.

Hinker's goons weren't stupid enough to get close to him, so they'd just keep plugging away at the wall until they realized Jin was a lot more patient than they were.

It came with the territory.

He'd been a hitman for the better part of thirty years, which all came about due to his particular ability with weapons. He was fast. Deadly fast. Some of that was natural talent, but not entirely. Jin also had a hint of magic on his side. That was due to the fact that he was a djinn. Yes, a djinn named Jin. It was definitely the cause of ridicule during his younger years.

He wasn't the genie type, but rather the kind who could channel ink as a well of energy, assuming the ink was drawn properly.

Jin's was.

Most of his line had tattoos plastered over every inch of their bodies. He'd refrained from that practice, instead only having the ink running across his back and down his arms, on the underside. In other words, looking at him, you'd never have a clue Jin was a djinn, which in part was because of his name. It helped cut down on the teasing some. If anything, based on the fact that he wore a long overcoat, a cowboy hat, and used six-shooters, shotguns, and rifles as his weapons of choice, you'd probably think he was just some crazy dude who happened to love the romantic notion attributed to gunslingers in the Old West. Not romantic in *that* way.

Anyway, we're talking about the Old West in the Badlands, where there'd actually been a good many gunslingers. The Old West of the topside had surprisingly few compared to the stories that'd been told. Folks up there carried forth Netherworld history as their own, to fill in the gaps. That was a common thing with topsiders.

Jin had never been outside the Badlands, but he'd read the books whenever he could get his hands on them. He wasn't much into reading on electronic devices, though, and getting his hands on paperbacks from topside wasn't exactly an easy feat. Visiting there wasn't something allowed due to his profession, either, so all he had were the books he could garner. He'd gathered quite a few of them over the years. Looking at him, you wouldn't think he'd be an avid reader, but he was. He loved to read, especially when it came to history. Knowing the past allowed him a decent compass when it came to predicting the future.

Most of the time it worked, too, especially when it came to firefights like the one he was presently enduring.

More bullets hit the plaster in front of him.

He sighed.

It'd always been a dream of Jin's to go to the Overworld. He'd seen pictures of their beaches and the clear water of their oceans, some of which were in the books he'd gotten, but many were only available on his datapad. Technology was not something Jin Kannon enjoyed using, but even he had to admit it was a necessary evil.

Regardless, the pictures he'd seen of the lovely beaches around the world topside appeared to be a veritable paradise to someone like Jin. The merest thought of sitting alone on a sandy beach while watching the sunset brought him a level of calm nothing else could provide.

The bullets suddenly stopped.

That's when the whispering began.

It was the thing about having patience; it confused your opponents. They were used to something far different. To them, battles like this were an adrenaline rush, a hyped-up life-or-death situation that made them feel alive, in the moment, even if they were terrified.

Knowing it was Kannon who they were fighting likely doubled their terror.

It was sad, really. Jin wasn't after them. In fact, if they'd wisely laid down their weapons and run away, never to look back, he would've happily left them alone.

Killing for the sake of killing wasn't in his blood.

Jin needed just cause, or at least a contract, and even those contracts had to come with a solid reason that pointed in the same direction as his moral compass.

"I'm not here for any of you," he declared. The whispers stopped. "Hinkers is using you as a stopgap so he can try to get away. He won't. Turds don't move fast enough." He paused, letting them ingest his calm, not to mention the fact that he'd just referred to their boss as a turd. It wasn't much, but mental games were typically more effective when you belittled the other guy. Knowing Jin held zero fear no doubt stoked their concerns regardless of the smack talk. Still, he liked fanning the flames wherever possible. "Even if the turd manages to get out of this building alive, I'll find him again. The unfortunate part is that all of you will end up dead while trying to protect him. And for what? Do you honestly think he's going to blink an eye over any of your deaths?"

There was no answer, of course.

"You're not even going to be given a proper funeral," he pointed out. "I mean, think about the dipshit you're working for, gang. We've already established he's a turd, right?"

More whispers.

"Yeah, we all know he's a turd. A big fat juicy turd." Jin began warming up his ink. "How many times has he given you a decent raise? How many times has he taken you out to dinner just as an atta-boy? I'll bet never." Silence. "And yet here you are doing your best to protect him. I mean, let's be real, if your dog dropped a deuce as big as Hinkers in your neighbor's yard, and your neighbor came out with a shovel to clean it up, would you protect the turd? Cause, gang, that's basically what you're doing here."

Jin channeled his magic and felt his eyes begin to burn. There'd been a time when the practice hurt. That was many years ago. These days, it was almost like scratching an itch you struggled to reach. He wouldn't say it felt great, but it was like the burn you got when whiskey funneled down your throat. It stung a bit and then brought you warmth.

Within seconds, Jin knew the location of each of them. There were indeed seven, and their hearts were pumping frantically.

Gotta love magic.

"Now, I'll make it clear one last time. You know my reputation. I won't fire at anyone who drops their weapons and vacates the premises. I won't hunt you down, either. Leave now and you're free to go." After a few moments, he added, "And don't worry about anyone taking out hits on you. Everyone who will be a witness to your leaving will be dead soon, including the big turd I'm here to…well…shovel up."

"What are you doing?" a hissed voice said as the clanking of multiple guns sounded. Footsteps followed as Jin magically watched multiple heartbeats exit the area. "Cowards!"

There were three of them left.

"Your friends may be cowards," Jin stated, "but they'll live, where you brave—aka stupid—few will be entering the Vortex soon, and for what? Defending a turd, that's what."

"Shut up!"

Ah, the seeds of doubt had been planted.

"I'll give you a few more seconds to contemplate."

"SHUT UP!"

That was followed by more bullets pounding the wall. It was a fruitless gesture on their part, but there was little doubt it made them feel better to believe it may have some effect.

The moment there was the briefest pause in their firing, Jin cranked up his magic and made his move.

When he used magic like this, he ended up being nothing more than a blur to the eyes of most. The world slowed down for Jin, too, giving him a lot of leeway to make decisions. He could see the bouncing of their semi-automatics as they fired many steps behind his constantly altering position. Looks of rage plastered their faces, their minds assuredly assuming they'd actually had a chance at besting him.

Before they could even register their time had passed, however, Jin placed three bullets through the backs of their heads.

Each of them fell forward with a thud.

Jin then dropped his guns back into their holsters and sighed.

A few seconds later, he heard a click and immediately kicked off toward the back of the room, diving over a large table while pulling it with him. If he'd not had his speed set to ten, he would've been visiting the Vortex next to those he'd just ended.

Fortunately, the table had taken the majority of the blast, only allowing a few bits of shrapnel through. Those pieces peppered Jin's jacket but caused him nothing but minor flesh wounds. It stung, of course, it just wasn't deadly.

"Fuck!"

That was Hinkers, who had clearly recognized he'd missed.

The turd had taken up a position to wipe Jin out himself, using his men as bait. That was dumb, but it'd also proved the point Jin had been trying to make to the goons before killing them. Hinkers, and all those like him, never gave two shits about the people who served to protect them.

What bothered Jin most was that he'd not picked up Hinkers' heartbeat. That'd only happened because Hinkers had stationed himself upstairs and far enough away, but Jin should have scanned a wider area before making any moves. It was reckless. Something like that tended to end the career of an assassin. Thankfully, Jin's career was nearing its end anyway, assuming he was able to complete this contract.

He would.

He always did.

Before moving this time, he did a detailed scan of the area. Hinkers and three others were standing on the platform directly above him. Scanning even further brought up nothing.

The rest of the area was clear.

"You missed, Hinkers. Mostly, anyway."

"You're still alive?"

"What gave it away? My ability to speak, maybe? Or are you capable of talking with the dead? I don't know how turds work, Hinkers, but I'm pretty sure they can't speak with the dead."

"If you don't stop calling me a turd I'm going to kill you."

"You're doing great so far…turd."

"You're the turd!"

"Nice comeback."

Jin got up and brushed off his outfit. There were more holes than he'd expected. That didn't make him happy. He grabbed his hat off the ground and gave it a quick study. Thankfully, it was fully intact.

"Do you have any idea how much it costs to have these jackets made?"

"Screw you, Kannon!"

"No time for that, I'm afraid," Jin quipped. It was weak, but whatever. "It's getting close to five o'clock. I have a meeting with my handler, and I intend on delivering this contract as solidified tonight."

Rapid footsteps and dropping weapons sounded from above.

"Get your asses back here!"

Jin cracked a smile. Hinkers' fear was palpable and his sole heartbeat told the story of someone who'd just been abandoned.

Moving quickly, Jin stepped on the side of the overturned desk and leaped up to grab the ledge above him. Flipping over the rail, he spun to find himself standing a few feet away from his mark

Hinkers wasn't your standard mob boss. He was short, scrawny, had a bald head and wire-rimmed glasses. He wore a white shirt that was buttoned to the top and his pants—though likely soiled—were personally tailored. They probably had to be, given his diminutive stature.

But Jin knew the real person behind the mask. The guy was a ruthless and sadistic killer.

While Jin killed as part of his job, he had rules about who he would target. Hinkers wasn't like that. He was the type who found pleasure in killing and torturing. Contracts on people like him were the kind Jin actively sought.

It made the assassin feel like he was at least doing *some* good for the world, even if his profession wasn't exactly tasteful.

"It's over, Hinkers."

The crime boss brought up a knife and held it out threateningly.

Jin glanced at the blade and then back up at the little man.

"Really?"

Obviously recognizing it was a stupid move on his part, Hinkers threw the knife over the railing and held his hands out.

"Listen, Kannon. You don't have to do this."

"Kinda do," Jin countered. "It's my job. Besides, you're a piece of shit—or a turd, I suppose, since we've been going with that descriptor. It's not as if the world really needs people like you around, you know?" He brought up his gun. "But, hey, here's something to take with you to the Vortex…you're my one thousandth confirmed contract."

"Ummm…yay?"

"Hinkers, that's *good* news—for me, anyway. It means I'm getting out."

He stepped forward.

"Wait—" said Hinkers, holding out his hands in desperation.

Jin didn't.

CHAPTER 2

Jin

Jin sat across from Chancellor Frey, the head of the Badlands Assassins Guild. She wore standard assassin's garb, which consisted of leathers, thin chainmail gloves, and knee-high boots—the magical kind that didn't make a sound when you walked across hard flooring. Her color scheme was red, which matched her hair and heavy lipstick.

If Jin hadn't known better, he would've expected her to be working a street corner in Infernal City.

Not that he would ever dare say such a thing to her. For one, it'd be beyond rude. More importantly, though, he would've ended up with his head on a stick. While Jin was more advanced than most when it came to killing, nobody was even close to the skills possessed by Chancellor Frey.

"I believe congratulations are in order, Jin," she said

with a genuine smile. "It's a rarity for any of our order to reach one thousand confirmed kills." She glanced away with a sigh. "Most die long before hitting such an achievement."

It was true. Jin had lost a good many friends in this job. In fact, after about two years he stopped allowing himself to get close to anyone.

Frey smiled again. "You, however, have made it, and that means you're done."

"Yes."

"Now, you may always reenlist for another thousand kills, should you so choose, but I have the feeling you've lost a bit of fervor for your role here."

"I have."

She nodded. "I fully understand. Still, there are many other positions you could hold in our illustrious organization." Jin wasn't sure he would've used that particular adjective. "Trainer, for one. Having someone with your level of expertise guiding our newer recruits would be a boon to the craft."

He'd thought about it, actually. There were many tricks of the trade that could save a life or two along the way. The problem he'd always had was knowing he'd start to care about the students, and even with his tricks and experience to help guide them, most would end up in the dirt before long. Worse, there were very few assassins who held out for contracts that targeted truly nefarious people. Training someone to take the life of an innocent target simply because someone didn't like said target was almost as bad as pulling the trigger himself.

Jin couldn't be a party to that.

"I don't think that's for me, Chancellor."

The look she gave him made clear she understood his position. Everyone knew she was amazing at reading people, which was one of the primary reasons her record remained untouchable in their field.

"Again, I get it." She leaned back in her chair and tilted her head at him. "Well, then?"

Jin had known the question was coming but he still had no real answer to give. Well, technically, he *did* have an answer, but she'd never go for it, so he'd racked his brain over the last year to come up with alternatives.

One option was to merely ask for enough money to allow him to travel the Badlands. But he knew that wouldn't last long. For one, he already had more than enough money to last a lifetime, so why ask for more? More importantly, though, was the fact that there weren't a ton of sights and the beaches here were kind of crappy. In other words, Jin would ultimately find himself sitting around doing nothing. That'd be bad for a guy like Jin since he'd likely end up with a bottle in his hand.

Soon, people would be calling him, "Jin the djinn who has a problem with gin."

He didn't want that.

Jin either needed to have a full life of vacationing or he needed to work. Work sounded like the better option, but he could pick up odd jobs from place to place. Travel had to be the priority.

Unfortunately, his true desire was off the table. It was too dangerous. *He* was too dangerous.

JOHN P. LOGSDON & JENN MITCHELL

Still, it *was* what he wanted, and he couldn't help but think it'd be smarter to ask and hear "no" than to never ask and to forever wonder if it *had* been possible.

Steeling his nerves, he said, "Well, I've always wanted to go topside."

"To do what?"

She hadn't even hesitated. That was strange. He'd thought certain she would laugh, call him a nut job in a colorful way, and then tell him to be serious.

"I...uh...to travel?"

"Hmmm."

What the hell? She appeared to be genuinely considering it.

While all the Assassins Guild documentation said you could do whatever you wanted if you hit the one-thousand confirmed kills in this gig, something the drafters of said articles must have recognized very few would achieve, they couldn't have meant *anything,* at least not literally. Besides, those who managed to achieve it always seemed to stay within the industry, doing one thing or another to continue their support of the cause. It was almost expected.

"Travel and then come back? Or did you have other plans?"

"Chancellor, I truly hadn't expected you to even entertain the idea, so I'm not sure what to say right now."

She laughed. "You signed a document that said you'd have the option to do whatever you chose, within reason, if you succeeded at hitting our primary objectives. You hit them, Jin."

"Yeah, I know. It's the 'within reason' part that made me assume topside was an impossibility."

"Impossible is not something people in our profession typically hear."

She opened her datapad and began scrolling around.

"The sticking point is to put people into situations that…" She paused. "Hmmm, this is interesting." She peered up at Jin. "How would you feel about hanging out at the beach in California?"

His heartbeat picked up. "You mean like the place in the pictures?"

"Yes, those."

"I've always thought that would be amazing if I'm being honest." A hint of melancholy struck him. "Sitting on the beach watching the sunset has been a dream for years."

"Okay then, one more question, and it's a doozy."

Jin sat forward. "Yes?"

"I know you've spent your entire life as an assassin, so this may come across as super weird to you." She chuckled as she glanced at the screen again. "It certainly would to me."

"Go on?"

"All right, Jin Kannon, an assassin who has achieved *Platinum-Ask-Status*, that of one thousand confirmed kills, how would you like to move topside and become the new Chief of the San Diego Paranormal Police Department?"

He gulped.

"No shit?"

"No shit. All you have to do is deal with a full integration cycle, have a number of memories baked into your skull, lower your ability to kill—though you'll still be solid enough to work as a cop, I would hope— and take an oath that you'll do your damnedest to protect the innocent, no matter the personal cost."

He gulped again. "Integration cycle?" It *was* the scariest part, though being a cop at all sounded like more work than he was interested in. But if it gave him the ability to go topside, it'd be worth it. He hoped that was true, anyway.

"It's admittedly the worst part...probably." She leaned forward, opening her eyes a bit more. "Well?"

"Um...can I have some time to think about it?"

Frey glanced back down at the datapad. "There are currently seventeen applications for the job and they're making a final decision any moment now, so no. If you want it, it's yours, but I have to get on with them now so I can make the necessary arrangements." She raised an eyebrow at him. "It takes you topside and puts you right by the ocean."

"Right."

She glanced at her watch. "I'll give you two minutes."

"Generous."

"Sorry."

It *did* sound amazing to Jin, aside from the part about him having to be a cop. Then again, would that be so awful? He'd effectively acted in a role that took out bad guys for years. Would this be much different?

Probably.

Still, there was the beach and topside and...well, dammit, when would someone like Jin Kannon ever get an opportunity like this again?

He sat forward, more worried than he'd been in a very long time, but also more excited.

"Yes. I'll…" He cleared his throat and let out three quick breaths. "I'll take it."

Frey gave him a look. "You're sure?"

"Not at all, but I'm damn well going to do it anyway."

CHAPTER 3

Raina

*R*aina Mystique had been second-in-command at the San Diego Paranormal Police Department for the last two years. She loved the job, but she would've admittedly loved pretty much any job. That's what happened when you were born a unicorn, it gave you magic along with a rosy outlook. Well, except during a full moon, but that wasn't for another couple of days.

She preferred not to look at the lunar calendar as it caused undue stress. Besides, everyone else on the team always reminded her anyway. Not that they needed to. The effects of a full moon on a unicorn were less than fun.

With a sigh, she looked at her badge and perked up again. Seeing her own smiling face reminded her that being happy was a choice, not a set of circumstances. The picture was a bit dated, but she still had blond hair and purple eyes. She'd gotten rid of the glitter long ago, though. Oh, the glitter showed up whenever she morphed into her horse form, but she only did that when absolutely necessary. Being in unicorn mode gave her far more attention than she enjoyed.

"All right, gang," said Chief Fysh as she walked into the debriefing room, "we've got our final selection for my replacement." She was holding up her datapad while looking as perfect as ever. Not only was she tall and lean, but she walked with a sway any other creature would be absolutely incapable of mimicking, and that's even when she was using her human form—which she always did unless she was in the water. Mermaids tended to be gorgeous until they were laughing maniacally at you as your ship crashed upon the rocks. Chief Fysh had never played that game, though. She'd always considered it boorish. "His name is Jin Kannon, he originates from the Badlands, and he spent the last twenty years as an ass…" She paused and squinted at the datapad.

"He was an ass?" asked Rudy. "How does a guy go about getting a job like that?"

"Right?" That was his partner, Clive.

Clive and Rudy were an odd pairing, though it could be argued there weren't any normal partnerships on the San Diego PPD.

Rudy was a wererooster, meaning he could shift into the shape of a rooster at will. That may not sound very useful but in San Diego, there were areas where chickens ran around on the street. While you could have a certain number of chickens legally, having too many was illegal. They never exacted fines on people, but the normals enforced the removal of any chickens beyond the allowable amount. The reason for this was to cut down on cockfighting, something Rudy used to excel at for obvious reasons. San Diego had a number of sections that weren't policed at all, however, specifically those inhabited by the local cartel. Standard cops steered clear of those areas and that meant chickens ran around in an almost "free range" situation. Translation: Rudy could shift and find himself in the mix of a bunch of chickens, overhearing conversations left and right without the bad guys knowing someone was eavesdropping.

Clive was a centaur…sort of. He'd inherited the human parts of both his mother and father, which basically made him less of a centaur and more of just a regular guy. Though, not quite. He *did* end up getting a few Centaurian perks—depending on your perspective. First was his ability to neigh really loudly; so loud, in fact, that he could pretty much make you shit yourself. The second was his massively muscular upper body. The guy was ripped. In contrast, his legs were spindly at best, which was a strange juxtaposition. The third inherited trait was his mane of hair. It was thick and luxurious. It was also a nightmare to maintain, requiring daily brushings to keep it shiny. The final thing he'd gotten was his centaur-sized, magical tail. It was stupidly large when Clive had it out. He could make it appear and disappear at will. Rudy once remarked the tail was so impressive that it had its own gravitational pull, using a crass descriptor by calling it "Clive's personal black hole." Now, having access to a tail of such size may seem pointless to most, but Clive had learned many useful purposes for it, including combat, pole vaulting, increasing his running speed, and creating mini-tornados.

Raina had always found it interesting that she couldn't see Clive's tail unless he brought it out for an appearance.

It was strange.

Not as strange as Clive's leather fetish, but that was another story.

"Ah, sorry," Chief Fysh said finally. "My datapad locked up. I meant to say he was the Assistant Magistrate."

Rudy nodded at Clive. "That makes more sense."

"Except that he remained an assistant the entire time."

"That's what I was after thinkin'," agreed Lacy, the team's leprechaun. She was about a foot tall, somewhat pudgy, had rosy cheeks, and drank like a sailor. She could fulfill wishes like most legends claimed, but only if she chose to do so, or was forced. It'd happened before. Lacey was best at sending out bursts of magic that would spin your head around. She also had a bluntness about her that Raina appreciated. Not many people did, but Raina found Lacy's refusal to pull punches refreshing in a world that Raina deemed too politically correct. Her green hair was always mussy when she wasn't wearing one of her ivy caps. "Must be a moron or somethin'."

"I don't believe so." That was Chimichanga, though everyone called her Chimi. Like pretty much everyone else at the San Diego precinct, she wasn't your standard super. She came from the only remaining community of cyclopses in the Netherworld. They were a protected species, which had made it a challenge for her to get a posting in the PPD at all, especially topside, but ultimately it was allowed because the cyclops elder rolled a few rocks against the wall during a solar eclipse and believed the positions they landed proved Chimi should be allowed to pursue her dream. Chimi's primary use to the force came with her incredible strength and an ability to focus like nobody's business. That had to do with her single eye. Due to the magic collar she always wore, normals never saw that gigantic eye like the supernatural community could. To them, she appeared to have the standard two-eye set. Chimi was one of Raina's favorites, though it was always a struggle when her cyclops friend delved into an astrology reading. "According to my readings, the new chief is exceedingly intelligent. Probably the smartest person in existence! You see, I woke up at 6:08 this morning. Now, if you divide six by two, you get three. Then if you multiply eight by two and subtract two from that, you get fourteen. That means we have three twos being used, which, if added together, equals six. If that doesn't make clear this new chief has an intellect that exceeds our greatest thinkers, I don't know what does."

The entire group stared at her with confused looks for a few moments.

"Right," Chief Fysh went on. "Anyway, he's going to be here around noon or so. I have a few things to clear up, then I'm going to go for a quick swim at Sea World. When I get back, I'll introduce Chief Kannon around and do the final handoff to him." She scanned the room and sighed. "You all already know how I feel about you. We've worked well as a team and I'm proud to have been your leader all this time."

"Back at ya, chief!" Rudy said.

She smiled at him and then flicked around on her datapad again. "We've already done your individual reviews over the last few weeks, so that's set. All the other paperwork is complete, too." She looked up. "Don't worry, I'm not going to be too far removed from things. Remember, I'll be one of the new Directors for this precinct. While I won't be around all the time, I'll make myself available as needed."

With that, she gave them a nod and then left the room and headed back to her office.

Raina couldn't help but notice it'd grown quiet. Everyone was obviously sad to see Chief Fysh go, and there was little doubt they were all apprehensive about breaking in a new chief, but Raina tended to look on the bright side of things wherever possible.

As far as she was concerned, it was an exciting time.

CHAPTER 4

Jin

*H*e caught a transport to Netherworld Proper, deciding to bypass the quick jump options. It wasn't fancy, but it allowed him to see the Badlands from the vantage point of someone who was merely a traveler. There was no agenda other than to observe and enjoy.

The air-rail system was relatively new and hadn't quite caught on as its inventors and financial backers had hoped. Jin understood why. Aside from the fact that the ride was bumpy, the view was less than stellar. Most of what he saw was brown and barren, though there were a number of mountains to the north. They were nice to look at, but he'd seen them more times than he could count. What he'd hoped was to catch a glimpse of villages, Hellion castles, dragons flying around, and so on. Part of the rules of building the rails, however, was that they needed to be fully out of eyeshot of most major areas.

Still, it was nice to take the slow route for once.

Jin's life had been filled with haste, purpose, and too much living in the shadows. Sitting in the first-class compartment of this train, even with its cruddy view, was a number of steps above his many years playing the role of a hitman.

When the train finally approached the wall that separated the Badlands from Netherworld Proper, Jin was presented with a beautiful view of the masterful construction. It alone was almost worth the ticket price. The wall was gigantic, rising up so high as to nearly touch the clouds. There was supposedly magic involved that extended the separation even further, but Jin was unable to see that. Obviously, the train was allowed to pass through the magic, proving the builders of the system had heavy backers indeed.

Once they'd gotten to the other side, a sea of cities appeared below. Either the residents of Netherworld Proper weren't worried about eyes from on high or there wasn't an option to fly around in order to reach their intended destination. Based on everything he'd read about their sister city, Jin assumed the former since the elders who lived here were known to consider themselves above the law.

He'd barely had the chance to take in even a few of the sights before the train pulled into a building and began to slow down.

"We have arrived at the primary nexus in Netherworld Proper," announced a woman's voice over the speaker. "Please make sure to take all of your belongings with you, if you are departing here. Our next stop will be the western nexus."

He got off the train and found himself standing in the middle of a bustling building that housed a massive shopping complex. There were far more people than Jin was used to and it put him somewhat on edge.

"Calm down, Jin," he whispered to himself. "You're no longer part of the game. Take a deep breath and head to the integration facility, just like we planned."

It wasn't a common thing for Jin to talk to himself, but it was also rare for him to leave the Badlands, be dropped off in the middle of loads of people, get a full integration, and then head off to topside in order to become the new chief of a police force.

Frankly, it was almost too much to take.

Jin wasn't shaken easily, especially after all the years he'd faced incredible odds while putting his life on the line, but this kinda sucked.

Was he making the right choice here?

He found a wall and slammed his back against it, fighting to keep calm. It took more than a few deep breaths, truth be told. Jin wanted to feel the steel of his guns, but they were packed away, deep in his luggage.

Then a thought struck and he reached into the smaller pack he was carrying.

Jin took out his dusty datapad and stared down at the opening screen. It showed an image of a sandy beach with crashing waves and a setting sun.

Instant peace flowed through his veins.

He could do this.

Raising his head, he glanced around to find a sign that pointed toward the integration building. As luck would have it, there was also a lull in bodies, giving him just enough time to drop the datapad back in its pouch before dragging his luggage toward his destination.

The place looked like your standard-issue government building. Jin couldn't explain why he'd expected it would be classier than offices on the Badlands side of the wall, but it wasn't. It was stark white with marble floors. There was a counter with a curmudgeon of a man staring at him.

Jin walked up and tipped his hat toward the guy.

"Name?" the clerk said, clearly bypassing formalities.

"Kannon. Jin Kannon. I'm…uh…here to—"

"Take a seat. You'll be called back in a few minutes."

The Jin of yesterday morning would've reached through and throttled the guy for being such a jerk, but as of last night, Jin had gained a different outlook on life.

Currently, that was based on willpower alone.

According to Chancellor Frey, the required changes Jin was due to face in this building as part of his request to live topside would change who he was at a fundamental level.

Thinking about that beach made him more than okay with that.

He took a seat and went to snag the datapad again, but there was no time.

"Jin Kannon?" a rotund lady called out.

He got up and headed her way. "That was quick."

"You're a special case, Mr. Kannon," she said. At least she was smiling, and it seemed genuine. Once the door closed behind them, however, her smile vanished. "Can't have two-bit killers sitting amongst the law-abiding populace, now can we?"

"I…uh…huh?"

She pointed at the wall. "Leave your bags there. Someone will be along to sanitize them and make sure you're not bringing any unauthorized paraphernalia into the Overworld."

"My guns are in there."

"And they'll remain in here unless you're planning to be a police officer, Mr. Kannon."

"Actually, I am."

She rolled her eyes and then looked down at her datapad. Her eyebrows arched. "Oh, it seems you are."

"I know."

"Well, my apologies then." Her attitude changed yet again. "And a chief at that, it seems."

"Hard to believe, right?"

"California?"

"San Diego, yes."

Her face began to glow and she looked at Jin with a newfound smile. "Always wanted to go there, Mr. Kannon. I daresay I'd even be willing to play a little fun-fun under the covers, should someone be willing to pay my expenses."

He grimaced at her. "Um…I…no?"

Her sour look returned and she pointed at the chair in the middle of the room. "Take your clothes off—all of them—and sit in that chair."

"All of them?"

"Did I stutter, Mr. Kannon?"

Once the door shut behind her, Jin let out an exasperated breath and began to disrobe. It'd only been less than a day, but it was clear he was out of his element. How was it that Jin Kannon, the guy who had been confirmed to have killed one thousand people, was the least rude person here? Was it because they hated their jobs so much and he'd actually kind of enjoyed his?

It may sound odd to hear someone like Jin actually enjoyed being a hitman, but he did. Sure, there'd been times when it hadn't been all that great, but he always knew where he stood. He never relied on anyone but himself—after the first ten or so targets were eliminated, anyway. The pay was decent and the benefits were great. Plus, with the number of contracts coming across the wire daily, Jin rarely suffered boredom, even with the exacting requirements for the jobs he would take.

He finished disrobing and sat on the cold chair. It was covered with plastic. Above him was an apparatus that resembled a salon-style hair drier. It lowered, covering his head and face like a full helmet would.

"Please place your hands on the armrests," said a computerized voice.

The moment Jin complied, straps locked his arms in place. His legs were soon strapped in as well.

Jin had fully expected that to happen, having read up on the procedure the night before, and so he relaxed into it.

"Mr. Kannon," the computerized voice said again, "you are about to undergo the entrainment phase of the integration cycle. Since you are requesting to leave behind your life as an assassin and enter a new life as an upstanding police officer, you will have a number of old memories selectively dulled. Do you comply?"

Frey told Jin he'd be asked this question, and it would prove to be the moment of truth. If he refused, they'd let him back out and he'd have to head home to the Badlands; otherwise, his new life topside would be kicked off.

"Do you comply?"

"Y…yes."

"I sense discontent, Mr. Kannon. Please affirm your desire to shift to a new life."

Part of the challenge of making such a big change was overcoming fear. Someone like Jin shouldn't have *any* fear, and when it came to facing hordes of soldiers or guards with weapons, he had zero. But he was facing something new here, something entirely foreign to how he'd spent his entire existence.

"Mr. Kannon, please affirm or decline your desire to shift to a new life."

It was time to shit or get off the pot. Was he going to go back to being a hitman or was he going to live near the beach and become a cop?

The cop idea wasn't great, obviously, but the beach…

"Mr. Kannon, please—"

"I confirm," Jin interrupted, steeling his resolve. "Let's do this."

"As you wish, Mr. Kannon. You will feel renewed and refreshed at the end of the cycle. Everything that happens during this level of integration will be deemed confidential. Please note that you may become slightly disoriented. This is normal. However, if you find yourself

JOHN P. LOGSDON & JENN MITCHELL

agitated or wracked with a sudden desire to soil yourself, please let us know. We hope you enjoy your entrainment procedure."

Everything went silent for a few moments before Jin heard the sound of classical music in the distance.

CHAPTER 5

Raina

They stayed in the conference room for a while, discussing the new chief. Each of them had their datapads open, searching for as much information as they could find, but most of it seemed to be fluff.

"Says here, this idiot basically was after performin' weddins," said Lacy. "I don't get how ye go from sayin', 'Do ye take what's her face to be yer awfully wedded wife?' to sayin', 'Get yer filthy paws up against the wall before I gut ye like a worm-filled hog.' Seems outta the realm of believability, it does."

"I think you meant 'lawfully wedded wife' there," suggested Chimi.

"I know what I was after meanin', ye single-eyed fiend."

Raina leaned back and pursed her lips. "There must have been more duties than that in his job; otherwise, I hate to say I have to agree with Lacy."

"Why do ye hate agreein' with me?"

Ignoring the question, Raina went on, "I do see case filings here where he had to weigh in on small civil claims."

That still didn't seem like a history that warranted him becoming a chief in the PPD. There had to have been more to him than what they were finding.

"Wait." Rudy leaned forward and blinked a few times. His head jerked in rapid fashion for about ten seconds. That typically only happened when he saw something exciting or if he was eating, and even then it typically only happened when he was in rooster form. "Could this be the same guy?"

He flicked his fingers a few times. The lights in the room went off and the contents of his datapad appeared on the far wall. It showed the video of a man who looked awfully similar to the Jin Kannon they were going to be reporting to soon.

Kannon was still for about three seconds before his eyes turned red. Then he became a blur as a few bodies dropped. After that, the video turned to static an instant after those red eyes appeared in full frame.

"What the hell was that?" asked Chimi. She rarely used any coarse language, including the word "Hell."

"I'm after knowin' exactly what that is." They all looked at Lacy and found her face was one of shock and awe. "This fucker weren't no assistant magistrate. He was after bein' an assassin in the Badlands."

That shut everyone up for a full minute.

Chimi was the first to move, pulling out a small velvet satchel that contained rocks, coins, tiny cards, and bones of some sort. She grabbed the cards and shuffled them. She then began placing three of them facedown on the table.

Carefully, she flipped over the first one. It showed the image of a coyote howling at the moon. The second one displayed two fish jumping up a rushing stream. The third was a red diamond.

Chimi crossed her arms and let out a slow breath. She appeared relieved.

Lacy, who generally used floating as her means of travel, hovered next to Chimi's gigantic head. "Well?"

"We have nothing to worry about. Jin Kannon is as harmless as a flea."

The team groaned.

"Great," said Rudy, "we have a fuckin' assassin as a boss."

Chimi frowned at him. "No, the cards say he's basically harmless, aside from passing judgment on civil cases and performing wedding ceremonies, anyway."

The rest of the team knew better. Chimi had nearly a one hundred percent track record of being absolutely wrong with her readings. She was so bad at it, in fact, the crew had learned to depend on it. If she said it was going to be a beautiful sunny day, everyone wore raincoats and boots. If she said there was zero chance of snow—in San Diego, mind you—they all put on their winter coats.

"Yer a doll, Chims," Lacy said, patting her on the shoulder. "Don't ever change."

"Why would I change?"

"So why are we all feeling this way?" Raina asked. "I

35

mean, we would prefer someone who knows how to fight over someone who doesn't, right?"

Clive sniffed and shook his head. "Were you watching the same video we just watched? What you just saw was a guy who was so fast the camera couldn't pick him up."

"Okay?"

"Imagine he tells you to get his coffee and you give him grief about it." Clive's face fell. "You'd be dead before you could blink!"

"Or at least before you could add two sugars and a splash of cream," agreed Rudy. They looked at him in confusion. "What? Looks like the kind of guy who takes his coffee with two sugars and a splash of cream." He cleared his throat. "Anyway, there's no way anyone in the Netherworld would allow a Badlands assassin to come topside, let alone put him in charge of a frickin' precinct. Right? I mean…RIGHT? No way."

The voice of Chief Fysh caused them all to jump. "Unless he goes through a full integration, which was a requirement." She sighed. "I suppose I should've known better than to assume this team would be satisfied with the story about him being an assistant magistrate. You're too good at your jobs for that."

"We are?"

"Yes, Lacy, you are." She leaned back against the wall. "Look, guys, Kannon hit a major milestone as an assassin —his one thousandth confirmed kill…"

"Holy shit," rasped Rudy.

"…which means he was given the option of what he wanted to do with the rest of his life. He chose to work for the PPD, and they have a rule in the Badlands

Assassins Guild that states you can do whatever you choose if you reach one thousand confirmed kills. It's in their bylaws and there's little that lies outside the scope of their reach."

Clive put his datapad down. "So to speak."

"Just because he can make such an ask, however, doesn't mean there aren't rules in fulfilling the request." Fysh gazed around at their faces. "Again, he's going through a full integration. He'll get new memories, have some old ones fuzzed out, and he'll have his abilities diminished to the point where they're appropriate for any cop in the PPD." She then gave Rudy a disappointed look. "And killing you over coffee? Really?"

"Some people take their coffee seriously, chief."

"You're overthinking it." Chief Fysh swept the room again. "You're all overthinking it. I've been assured he'll be perfect for the job. If he's not, he'll go through reintegration again and again until he is, or until he decides to choose a different path." She turned to walk back out of the room but stopped and glanced back. "Remember, he works for me now. Do you honestly think I'd be stupid enough to allow a full, unaltered Badlands assassin to take my place?"

Nothing more needed to be said.

CHAPTER 6

Jin

The light show and music were overwhelming. Jin assumed that was the intention since it came with tons of whispering words. Keep the mind active in one way while feeding it loads of data through the backdoor.

Sitting naked made him concerned about using that particular term.

"Normals are your friends. You would never wish to harm a normal. Your purpose is to protect normals, along with your own kind. But should push come to shove, you will protect the life of a normal over the life of a super. This is your role as a police officer and you are proud of this fact."

He'd met very few normals in his life. They were a rarity in the Badlands. Those he'd met had been less than impressive, even if they carried enough clout to allow them a trip to the Netherworld. Everyone knew the toughest normal would easily fall to the wimpiest super. It was a simple case of physics. Now, if there were weapons involved, there was the possibility of an incredibly skilled normal winning a bout against a crappy super.

And Jin supposed that was the point of why his new role in the PPD was so important, and he *was* proud that he'd be in the position to protect normals wherever possible.

Jin blinked at the thought.

That was quick.

Minutes ago his brain never considered that watching over normals was going to be such a big deal. Now, it wasn't only important to him, it was becoming *very* important.

Well, good.

Right?

Yes, it *was* good. Great, in fact. He was Jin Kannon, the protector of the people!

Wow.

Okay, this was getting a bit strange now.

"Mr. Kannon, please relax and allow the process to take effect."

He had to do just that. Jin was so used to having his guard up that he was struggling to let it down at all, even though it was clear this integration thing was working regardless.

"Focus on the music, Mr. Kannon."

That was the purpose of it, obviously, so he did as he was told. The string section had always been Jin's favorite, especially when a solo violin or viola was playing. It brought him peace for some reason. Normally, he would listen to rock music that came from topside. That *was* one thing normals tended to do better than supers. This music, though, was nice. Active. It had a gentle cadence that was causing him to drift off into a dreamlike state until everything went dark.

And then ... BOOM, the music struck with a set of storm drums that nearly launched Jin directly from the chair. If straps hadn't been holding him down, he probably would've launched it across the room.

Lights were filling his vision, causing him to squint.

"Mr. Kannon, this step of your integration is complete, though you will need to return every few months for reintegration as your particular case requires it."

"Okay," he mumbled, feeling quite groggy.

"Please note that you have indeed soiled yourself."

"I did?"

"Worry not, Mr. Kannon. This is a common occurrence, which is why we use the protective plastic on the chairs." The straps fell off his arms and legs as the helmet lifted off his head. "If you would kindly go to the room ahead and to your left, you will be thoroughly cleaned."

With a grimace, Jin pushed himself up and duck-walked across the room, feeling like a complete buffoon.

The door sealed behind him and he was hit with a blast of cold water that came in from every imaginable angle. It felt like he was being put through a human carwash, which included robotic brushes and soap streamers. But it was the cold water that sucked the most. It was arctic cold.

Thankfully, as soon as the washing was done, a drying

system flipped on, blowing toasty warm air. It hadn't lasted long enough to warm Jin completely, but at least he'd stopped shivering by the time he was dried.

A hole in the wall opened and his outfit was inside. "Please put on your clothes and go to the next station."

The process hadn't been fun, but Jin no longer questioned his decision. The fact that he could still remember he *had* been asking it was good. Also, Jin still knew he'd spent all his adult life as a hitman. He couldn't remember the details of any kills at the moment, though, except the last one. That was a bit disquieting, considering he had a decent memory when it came to how he'd ended his targets. Try as he might, though, the only one that held any clarity was Hinkers.

After slipping his boots on, Jin plopped his hat on and walked out the door and to the next room.

It was another chair, but this one didn't have any plastic on it. It was in the middle of a dark room with a white spotlight shining on it.

Taking the hint, Jin walked over and sat down.

"Shall we begin?" asked a man.

"Yes."

"As the sky spins in orbital ecstasy, how likely is the cow to expand upon algebraic platitudes?"

His brain scrambled. "Sorry, what?"

"How often are roses called to serve cheese to ambassadors?"

"Roses serve cheese to ambassadors?"

"If you rode a vehicle that had only three tires and four of those tires were flattened by a feather, how quickly would a lava flow melt against the rush of hatcheries?"

"I have no idea what you're talking about."

"Six pickles subtracted from one egg leaves how many perfume bottles?"

"Nine?"

Jin had no idea why he'd even attempted to answer that.

"Who entered a plea of guilty during the reign of vitamin indigestion?"

"Wait, I know this one." He didn't.

The man continued without waiting for Jin to even attempt an answer. "There are only four primary elements, including toes, trees, curtains, and loud noises. What is the fifth element?"

"You just said there were only four—"

The questions kept coming, each one leaving Jin more of a slobbering mess than the last.

Ten questions later he found himself hanging to the side, barely able to maintain his seated position as drool dripped from his lips.

Then, out of the blue, the man asked, "What is your favorite food?"

"Huh?" Jin's head immediately started to return to normal. "What?"

"What is your favorite food?"

He wiped his mouth off on his jacket and sat up, feeling like his world was reforming yet again.

"Uh…pizza."

"Do you have the desire to kill anyone?"

Aside from the people running the facility, he didn't have the desire to kill anyone. To be fair, though, Jin couldn't recall ever having the *desire* to kill anyone. Sure, there were times when he'd wanted to punch someone in the head but kill them. Nah. That only happened because it was his job.

He squinted and chewed his lip for a moment.

"Do you have the desire to kill anyone, Mr. Kannon?"

"No."

"Does the alignment of the planets have any bearing on events?"

"No."

"Does the position of the moon control light?"

"It can," Jin answered.

"How?"

"Via an eclipse. It can temporarily block the sun. It can also be positioned so that it reflects more or less sunlight depending on the day of the month."

There was a long pause as he tried to comprehend what the hell had just happened to him. He knew integration/reintegration cycles were hated, especially deep reintegrations, but up until today, he'd only heard or read secondhand stories. Now, he fully understood those people had not been exaggerating.

"You have completed this part of the integration cycle and your paperwork has already been completed for you, Mr. Kannon."

"Thank you."

"You may exit the room through the door with the blue light above it, collect your things, and be on your way."

"Right."

It felt like a three-mile walk to that door, but once Jin

got on the other side of it, he drew in a deep breath and decided to do his best to put that entire ordeal out of his memory.

CHAPTER 7

Hector

The new head of the cartel inherited the position after his father's passing, which had only happened a couple of weeks prior. Everyone was told to keep the transition under wraps, not telling the local community, until things stabilized.

It wasn't easy.

Their new boss was Hector Leibowitz. Yes, Leibowitz. It's complicated.

Unlike his father, Hector was someone who wasn't a huge fan of violence. It would be going too far to say that he abhorred it, but his preference was to minimize it wherever possible. Also, he was more positive than his father had ever been. Not to the extreme of someone like, say, Raina Mystique, but that's only because Hector wasn't a unicorn. He was part werewolf, part normal—his mother, Joan Leibowitz, was really into the *Twilight* books. The majority of the members of his cartel were either pure werewolves or half-werewolf/half-normal. Those books had a pretty large impact on how much "normal action" the werewolves in the area received for a few years.

It was funny how people Topside believed werewolves were simply normals who had suffered some kind of curse or something. Hector wasn't one hundred percent certain what they believed if he was being honest. Either way, topside beliefs over things like werewolves were largely incorrect. Werewolves were their own race. They originated in the Netherworld, the same as every supernatural race had done. Hector assumed the legends that were built topside came about because all shifters can *look* human, but they're not really human. They're merely in the shape of a human, and few would argue being in "human form" made certain tasks far simpler than being in "wolf form." The thing is that when in human form, any shifter is capable of procreating with a normal.

Sadly, in so doing, their offspring is considered impure.

Hector's chapter of the cartel, known as *The San Diego Dogs*, ruled the area, but that didn't mean they were the top dogs when it came to the entire organization. That title went to Mr. Becerra, who chose to remain south of the border while overseeing multiple cartels that ran along the southern edge of the United States, not to mention the ones in New York and New Jersey. He was a ruthless leader who expected all heads of his cartels to be equally ruthless. If they weren't, they were replaced. As tough as Becerra was, though, he also carried a fierce trait of loyalty. It was a dog thing. The thing was, he'd loved Hector's father dearly, treating him like a brother and calling him the only leader of the U.S. chapters who had any gumption whatsoever.

And so, with respect to the memory of Hector's father, Becerra made clear he would give Hector a few months to find his own ruthless streak instead of immediately replacing him with someone more sinister.

Hector feared that would never happen.

He just didn't have it in him. All of his life consisted of kindness and positivity. Sure, he'd been in fights and had even knocked in a few heads during his time in the cartel, but he never found joy in it.

Still, he had to at least adhere to the basic rules of the cartel in order to work on his not-exactly-a-tough-guy issues, and the first one was to kidnap the outgoing chief of the San Diego Paranormal Police Department.

It was a ritual that had become part of the chapter rules, a way to show the PPD that the cartels were not to be trifled with. The practice started roughly thirty years ago in Texas when the chief of the Laredo PPD announced he would be leaving. The guy had caused so much grief for the Laredo cartel that the moment he walked out the door on his last day, they put a burlap bag over his head, threw him into a van, drove him to an undisclosed location, and threw him into a cell, only giving him enough food and water to make it through each day. It had become a big stink that caused a year-long war between the PPD and the cartels. When the air cleared, the ex-chief was delivered back but the practice then continued, each time becoming less and less violent.

There was a lot of turnover when it came to PPD chiefs along the southern border.

Ultimately, it happened merely as a ritual, but it was an important one because the cartels had grown in power and income since the original event,

People like Becerra were superstitious. He firmly believed that stopping the practice would result in a reversal of luck the cartels had seen since that fateful day in Laredo.

In other words, Hector had no choice but to comply.

Word on the street was that Chief Frannie Fysh had been offered the role of Director, so she was the outgoing chief of the PPD. Nobody knew who her replacement was, yet, but that was a concern for another day. The only thing Hector had to worry about right now was continuing the kidnapping tradition.

And continue it, he would, but only in a way that *he* wanted it to go down.

"Okay, guys," he said, standing in front of his crew of ruffians, "you all know the drill. We have to kidnap the exiting chief. It's in our bylaws and Mr. Becerra expects it to happen." He put his hands up. "Now, I know you've all served my father for years, and I get that you have become used to a certain style of working your jobs. That's great. It's understandable. Habits are formed and they can be a doozy to break." Hector took a deep breath. "You're working for me now, though, and I'm expecting things to be done a bit differently."

His crew shifted on their feet, glancing back and forth at one another with looks of uncertainty.

He had to tread carefully or reports would start

flooding over to Becerra and Hector would soon find himself working as a ranch hand in the sweltering heat of Hermosillo, Mexico.

No, thank you.

"I'm not asking that any of you *not* do the job." Hector put on a fierce face that made clear he expected their best. "It must be done. Again, it's tradition." He softened slightly. "However, I want you all to at least *try* to do the job without causing any unnecessary harm to anyone involved."

The hand of his second-in-command, Sofia Rossa, went up. She was a tank of a soldier, short and stocky, arms filled with rippling muscles, and veins that bulged. Her hairstyle of choice was a spiked mohawk that had blood-red tips. She also had two scars on either side of her face, and both were self-inflicted, which she'd personally designed in order to put the fear of hell into anyone who faced her.

Hector felt that fear at the moment.

"Yes?"

"You want us to kidnap that chief bitch while not hurting anyone?"

"I want you to kidnap the chief…bitch…while *trying* not to hurt anyone." There was a distinction, but everyone still looked confused. "Look, guys, you're all seasoned warriors. Everyone knows that. You've got nothing left to prove. You've all got massive cojones. That's well-documented." He furrowed his brow at Sofia. "I mean, I know you don't literally have cojones, Sofia, but—"

"Yeah, I get it, boss. Go on."

"Right." Hector had to be careful here. "The point is

there's nobody questioning anyone's toughness. Why would they? You've proven yourselves time and again over the years." And here came the tough sell. "What I want to learn is how well you can *control* yourselves. Again, you're clearly beyond capable when it comes to running into battle with guns blazing, or knives flashing, or...well...whatever. But sometimes the best missions are those where nobody gets hurt."

"Where's the fun in that?" asked Cano, but the way his eyes were glancing around it appeared as if his words were merely for show. He was one of the newest members of the cartel, having only been part of the crew for about a year. He'd quickly risen up in the ranks to stand next to Sofia, though. Actually, almost everyone was certain they'd become an item. Looking at them standing side-by-side, you'd have thought they were twins, even if Cano was roughly three inches shorter than her. He then added, and it was clear he was forcing his enthusiasm while speaking, "Um...knocking teeth in is the part of this job that I like most."

"Yeah!" cheered the rest of the team.

Hector eyed Cano for a moment. It was obvious the man was playing a role more than speaking as his true self.

Regardless, Hector had been expecting there would be a backlash in response to his more relaxed plans for the kidnapping. It was an event *The Dogs* rarely got to participate in and they looked forward to making the most of it. Too bad for them Hector used to date Chief Frannie Fysh, meaning he wasn't going to allow them to do their usual pain and punishment techniques.

"I get it," he said. "I really do." He didn't. "You're all the best of the best when it comes to doing the worst of the worst. You have no equals."

That seemed to appease them somewhat, and that was the one thing his father had told him. "Make sure you keep the soldiers happy, boy, or you'll soon find yourself working in Hermosillo…or dead."

This was Hector's show now, though, and he was going to make some changes, even if it meant risking a trip to Hermosillo. Besides, he honestly believed his way was going to ultimately prove more beneficial to the business, not to mention the community at large. He had no intention of killing anyone with kindness, but he held the contention that true power came with self-control.

He forced his resolve and allowed himself to turn somewhat stern.

"You've all proven yourselves as excellent killers. Again, what I want to see now is how much control you have. If you can't control your lizard brains, you're of no use to me and you'll soon find yourselves working in Hermosillo."

It was worth a shot, even if nobody seemed to care about the threat.

Sofia was the first to nod. "I think I see what you mean, boss. You're saying there is more power in refraining than in letting go. As warriors, only pussies kill when they don't need to 'cause that just makes them nothing but shitty animals."

"Um…yes?"

"Yeah, I see what you're saying." Her nodding was much stronger now as she stepped over and stood next to

Hector, turning to face the rest of the crew. "You heard the boss. We're gonna kidnap the chief of the PPD and we're gonna do it without hurting the bitch. You feel me?"

Nobody was stupid enough to counter anything Sofia decreed.

"Then let's get the hell outta here and get it done," she bellowed and then quickly turned toward Hector, "assuming you're done with your flowery speeches and shit, boss."

Hector deflated a bit. "Yes, that'll do for now."

"Sweet." Sofia walked straight toward the soldiers, causing them to all step aside. "Let's ride, fuckers!"

CHAPTER 8

Raina

Chief Fysh came out to the main office area as everyone got back to their desks. Not a lot happened during the day in the PPD. Supers tended to cause problems at night more often than during lunch. It happened, but it was rare. The majority of the time, the officers didn't stumble into the office until around four in the afternoon.

That's not to say the place was left unmanned.

The station's AI was always on duty. His name was Rusty and he was the backbone of the branch. He acted as the connection point for all things, including incoming calls, and dispatch, as well as general communications and record keeping.

There was also the SD PPD's tech lead, Miss Kane. She had requested people refer to her as "Mistress," but the chief had nixed that requirement, so she settled for "Miss" or "Miss Kane," though "Ma'am" was also within her realm of acceptability. Miss Kane was a succubus, which was quite uncommon in the field of technology. It was kind of rare to see in the PPD at all. There were a couple of incubi in the Seattle PPD, but Raina had never formally met either of them. Miss Kane rarely hung around the precinct during the evening, having other pursuits on her mind, so most of her work was done during daylight hours.

This turned out wonderfully for Rusty because he was rather infatuated with Miss Kane, actually being the only one who called her "Mistress" at the office. When it came to her, Raina knew very well that all Rusty could think about was *sex*.

"Raina," Chief Fysh said, "I'm going to head over to Sea World for a quick dip. If you hear from Kannon before I get back, get in touch with me, okay?"

"You got it, Chief." As Fysh headed out, Raina called after her, "Have fun!"

"Brown noser," Rudy chided. "She's leaving, Raina. You don't have to kiss her ass anymore."

Clive leaned over. "Actually, I disagree. She's moving on up to the Director level, remember? If anything, a juicy smooch on her ass right now would probably be the smartest move."

"Good point," admitted Rudy. "Honestly, I wouldn't mind putting a juicy smooch on her ass, anyway."

"Right?"

Clive and Rudy high-fived because they were children.

Raina merely rolled her eyes and refocused on typing up her reports for last night. She knew who she was as a person. She was not brown-nosing. Raina simply liked to be nice and kind, wherever possible. Not only was it the proper thing to do, it often helped to make up for the few days out of each month when her dark unicorn came to life.

"*Hey, Raina,*" the voice of Rusty came in through her connector, "*got a sec?*"

"*Sure, what's up?*"

"*Well, it's coming on the fifth anniversary since I was installed by Mistress Kane, and I was wondering if you think I should maybe get her some kind of gift?*"

These kinds of conversations were awkward for Raina, especially since Rusty was a computer, but she refused to treat him any differently than she would anyone else. Was he sentient? That was something she couldn't answer easily. He *seemed* to be. She just wasn't an expert on that stuff.

"*Well, what kind of things does she like?*"

"*Whips, chains, ball-gags, rope, blindfolds, buttpl—*"

"*Right, right! I get it.*" She should never have asked the question the way she had. "*Let me try again. What kind of things does she like specifically as they relate to your relationship with her?*"

"*USB drives, viruses, surge protectors...well, surge 'unprotectors,' actually. She's also designed a software buttpl—*"

"*Sorry, what's a surge unprotector?*"

"*Oh, well, whenever she asks me for something that I can't deliver straight away, she sends a jolt through in order to punish me. It's delightful.*"

Raina wanted to say, "Ew," but didn't.

Still, it was awkward for a computer to be submissive to a succubus, or anyone for that matter. Then again, weren't computers basically tools to be used by humans? In many respects, they did play the ultimate submissive role.

She shuddered.

"What if you were to think of something a little more thoughtful? Something non-sexual."

"Hmmm. Let's see. She has mentioned a few times that her office is too bland. I suppose I could alter the tech bay to give her the ability to change the color on the walls or put up images or something."

"That sounds wonderful!" Raina loved the idea for herself, actually. *"If I were her, I'd find that to be quite the romantic gesture."*

"Really?"

"Absolutely. It's thoughtful, shows you care about her, and that you feel there's more to your relationship than power surges."

"You're the best, Raina. Thanks!"

Just as she said, *"Of course,"* Chimi walked up and said, "Can you get the chief on your connector? Mine's not going through."

Raina tried but it couldn't connect. That sometimes happened when a person went down to the main level. There were a number of stop points as you tried to enter or leave, and each one had signal-blocking installed.

"She's probably just trying to get out to her car, Chimi. Something I can do to help?"

"I just had a question about my review."

"Ah." She got up from her desk and headed into Chief Fysh's office. It was the only place on the floor where you could see directly down to the parking lot. "Let's see if her car's still here or not."

It was, but that wasn't what drew Raina's attention.

"Uh oh," said Chimi loud enough that everyone rushed into the room to see what was going on.

"Aren't those the cartel guys?" asked Clive.

"They are," replied Rudy, "and they're putting a burlap bag over the chief's head."

Lacy floated up next to Raina's head. "Looks like they're throwing her into that white van, too."

"Weird."

That's when Chimi took two large steps over to the little whiteboard on the wall that read, "It's been three years and six days since the chief has been kidnapped." She erased the "three years and six days" and wrote "zero days" in its place.

"Hey, gang," Rusty said through the loudspeaker, "I don't know if you know this already, but I just picked up Chief Fysh being kidnapped on the video feeds!"

"We know," they replied in unison.

"Then why aren't you doing anything about it?"

They all glanced around at each other, blinking.

Again, as one, they said, "Shit." Well, except for Chimi. She said, "Whoopsie."

CHAPTER 9

Jin

is head had finally cleared up as he jumped through the portal and arrived at the nearest station to the precinct. It was only a few blocks away. He thought it would be in the same building, but the general governmental populace considered themselves to be more important than the cops.

Seemed they always were.

What was interesting was how Jin instinctively knew precisely where to go when he stepped out onto the main sidewalk. They'd given him new ink on his left wrist, obviously taking care while adding it since only one of the lines merged with the tattoo he'd already had there.

On top of that, the closer Jin got to his destination the more anxious he became. It wasn't fear-based anxiety. It was more like the drive to get things done. He felt the growing urge to get to the PPD offices and take over his role as the chief.

It was kind of intense.

There was a pull toward the green building on his left. It looked clean and high-tech. To be fair, most of the buildings he saw around the area were nicer—or at least cleaner than what he was used to seeing in the Badlands. There'd been a few incredible structures down there, for sure, but not nearly as many.

A white van squealed out of the driveway to the right. Jin caught sight of a squat, tough-looking woman sitting on the passenger side. Her eyes locked on his for a moment. Something felt wrong about her. The feeling was justified a moment later as she gave him the finger when they sped on by.

If nothing else, it was nice to have at least *some* similarities between San Diego and the Infernal Strip in the Badlands.

Jin shook his head and walked up to the doors of the building.

Multiple guards stood around when he entered. They eyed him suspiciously for a moment, clearly summing up his threat level before returning to their normal duties. Jin had the feeling they hadn't considered him much of a threat. He probably should have felt somewhat slighted by that, but for reasons he could only attribute to integration, he didn't.

Strange.

He walked up to the guard at the main desk. The guy gave Jin a quick scan and a pleasant look.

"What's the purpose of your visit today, sir?"

"My name is Jin Kannon. I'm the new chief of the San Diego Paranormal Police Department."

The guy's eyebrows went up and all the guards seemed to snap to attention, saluting and everything.

Jin had to admit it kind of felt good to have a bit of recognition.

"Um…at ease." He wasn't sure what else to say.

They all relaxed.

The guard at the desk stood up and reached out his hand. "Guard Levi Snoodle is my name, sir. It's a pleasure to meet you."

Jin took his hand and nodded. "Are you all members of my team?"

"Not exactly, sir. We're working for a different division. However, most of us do hope to one day find ourselves in the PPD in some capacity or another."

"I see." He was sure there were political reasons he'd soon learn. "Well, this is my first stop from the Badlands, so I'm completely green with how everything works. I'm sure the current chief will explain it all to me in due time."

"As you say, sir." The man was tapping away at the datapad on the desk. He pointed to a spot on the desk. "Could you please place your wrist on the scanner, sir?"

Jin did as he was told.

"Perfect." He read the screen. "Okay, you should receive a contact via your connector."

A voice in Jin's head said, *"Welcome to the San Diego Paranormal Police Department, Jin Kannon. Please reply by stating your name so that our systems may acclimate to your voice profile."*

"Um…Jin Kannon."

"You have to say it via the connector, sir," the guard pointed out. "You kind of just think it."

He sighed, feeling the urge to get the process over with growing into an intense *need*.

"Jin Kannon."

"What was your previous job, Mr. Kannon?"

He blinked at that question. "*I want to say I was an Assistant Magistrate, but I know I was an ass—*"

"And how long were you in that position?"

"Twenty-three years, four months, nine days, and—"

"Your profile is complete."

There was a dinging sound that came from the guard's desk. "All set, sir." The guy stood up and pointed toward the back elevators. "You'll be heading up to floor number four. I've bypassed all the standard security screens since this is your first day."

Jin frowned at that, thinking it was an odd thing to do for someone they didn't know. One would imagine an unknown would get the deep-glove treatment. Not that Jin *wanted* that kind of thing, but it seemed less than secure not to cover all their bases. If he was going to be the guy running the show here, assuming he had any control at all over what happened on this floor, he wasn't going to tolerate lax procedures.

"Sorry," he said, even though his brain was burning to get to his new job, "shouldn't a new person to the scene be scrutinized more severely than someone who already works here?"

Snoodle's face turned red.

"I…uh…well, I hadn't considered…I mean…uh…"

"Relax," said Jin, putting his hands out. "Just set the machines however they're supposed to be. I'm not looking for special treatment." His brain begged to differ. It seriously wanted him to get upstairs NOW, and his active thoughts were desperately hoping there wouldn't be any literal deep-glove-style searches. "If anything, we should relax the standards on trusted personnel, not people you're meeting for the first time."

He was shocked to see that comment appeared to surprise the guard. "Woah. That actually makes a lot of sense, sir."

It seemed pretty obvious to Jin, but he'd not yet been fully acclimated to government life.

After a bit of work on his datapad, the guard pointed at the machine on the left. "Please put your bag there, sir, and then walk through the scanner."

Jin gave him a nod and did as he was told.

Buzzers went off almost immediately and all the guards pulled out their weapons and trained them on Jin.

He put up his hands.

"On the ground, dirtbag!" commanded Guard Snoodle. Jin grimaced at him and the guy quickly shook his head as the blood drained from his face. "Oh, crap. I'm so sorry, sir! It's my training. I would *never*—"

"Calm down," Jin interrupted, having gone through some pretty heavy conditioning himself not even two hours prior. "I'm carrying my guns. I can now see I should have left them in my luggage until being sworn into my new role." Slowly, carefully, he opened his jacket to reveal his weapons. "If you would like me to remove them and place them in my suitcase, I would be happy to do so." The sound of hands gripping guns even tighter filled the room, including Snoodle's. "Alternatively, if one of your guards would like to liberate the weapons from me and hold them until I'm officially sworn in as chief, that would be fine as well."

Their training had engaged, as it should have, and it was impressive. Jin mostly wanted to make sure his first day on the force wasn't also going to be the last day, especially since he hadn't even had time to actually *start* his first day.

One of the other guards inched over and pulled the guns free from their holsters. Jin felt his eye twitch as something deep in his subconscious mind ached to snap the guy's arm, whip out the guns, and unleash hell on everyone in the room, leaving nothing but a mass of bodies in his wake.

His mouth went instantly dry at the thought. That was coupled with a pain in the center of his forehead. It didn't feel good at all.

Woah.

Once the guns were off his person and safely tucked away in his bag, the guards lowered their weapons and looked around at each other in confusion.

Yep, training.

The next ten minutes consisted of Jin being scanned from head to toe, asked several questions from a computer terminal, having his retina and fingerprints checked against his Netherworld records, and being apologized to more times than he could count. It was a bit much, and Jin's anxiety continued to rise the longer it took to complete the transition phase from hitman to chief of the PPD. He had no idea why that was so damned important, but it was getting to the point where he was starting to sweat.

Finally, a green light went on and Guard Snoodle said, "You're all clear, sir. And, sir, again, I'm really really *really* sorry about what happened."

"Let it go, Guard Snoodle," Jin said as he entered the elevator. "You were just doing your job. Everyone was just doing their jobs."

The doors shut and he cracked his neck from side to side.

"It's barely day one, Jin, and things aren't exactly going smoothly." He breathed in deeply through his nose and released the air slowly through his mouth as the bell rang for the fourth floor. "The worst is behind us, though. Of that I'm sure. Your new life is about to begin and even though this morning has been filled with less-than-fun experiences, that's all in the past now."

The doors opened.

"Besides, what else could possibly go wrong at this point?"

CHAPTER 10

Jin

*J*in was greeted almost immediately by a tall, blond woman with purple eyes. There was something about her that seemed far different than anyone he'd ever met. Her eyes being purple was one aspect he'd not seen before, but there was something more to her that had him wondering.

"Jin Kannon?" she asked, sounding more cheery than any person should.

Was it her positivity? That wasn't a common theme amongst Badlanders, especially those who worked in his field. But there was more to it than that.

"Yes. Are you Chief…uh…" He quickly glanced down at his datapad, almost unable to function due to the need to complete the transition.

"Frannie Fysh," she answered. "And, no, I'm Deputy Chief Raina Mystique."

"Ah." Jin nodded, blinking rapidly while giving up on

what it was about her that seemed so strange. It wasn't strange in a bad way or anything, but it was definitely strange. Finally, his desire to know outweighed his urge to complete his mission. "You seem…different."

"I get that a lot," she replied, looking chuffed that he'd noticed. "I'm a unicorn."

"Oh wow."

She smiled even bigger. "I get that a lot, too."

That's when he realized he was being super awkward. "I'm sorry, I—"

"It's quite all right. My kind have that effect on people." She bobbed her head around for a moment. "Considering there are very few people like me—one, including me, unless there's someone I don't know about—it's quite acceptable the way people respond when we meet."

It probably wasn't, but he was getting close to falling over. "Well, it's very nice to meet you, Raina, but I really need to see the chief right now."

He was unable to control himself as he pushed past her and walked out into the main area to find everyone standing up, each obviously wanting to greet him. He couldn't handle that at the moment. If the baton wasn't passed soon, he was certainly going to lose his mind.

"But, sir—"

"The chief, please," Jin rasped as he glanced around, feeling as if he was a man in the middle of the desert who was begging for water. "Now. I need to see her now."

"Yes, sir, but she's—"

Jin saw the sign on a door that read *Chief Frannie Fysh* and rushed toward it, only to find the office empty.

"Dammit! Where is she?"

He spun around to find all their faces carrying a massive weight of concern. Crap. He'd gone and freaked them out. He hadn't meant to.

He just….

He just needed to tell them what the hell was going on.

Grabbing the nearest chair, Jin sat down and pulled his hat off, doing his best to fight away the gripping anxiety.

"I'm sorry, gang. Really. I don't know what the hell they did to me at integration this morning, but as I've gotten closer and closer to this building my brain has been burning more and more." He gritted his teeth. "I honestly feel like my head is going to explode if I don't get this transition over with pretty damn fast."

"Looks like they put a time lock on you," one of the officers announced from his desk. "Just checked the records. That's pretty messed up. They must have been afraid you'd go nuts topside or something."

"And I'm about to…" Jin glanced back at Raina. "Where is she?"

"That's what I've been trying to tell you, sir." Raina gulped and looked at the rest of the room for help. They all quickly glanced away. Nice. "Um…well…she…um…"

"Please just tell me, Deputy Mystique."

By way of answering, she pointed at the wall in the chief's office. Jin turned back and looked at a sign that said, "It's been zero days since the last chief was kidnapped."

He slowly turned back. "Huh?"

"She was kidnapped by the local cartel!"

Jin dropped his head into his hands and groaned. Of course, she got kidnapped. Why wouldn't she have? He never should've tempted fate by asking what else could possibly go wrong that day. It'd been a dumb question. In his previous life—which ended less than twenty-four hours ago—things went smoothly most of the time. Sure, he got shot at, had basically no friends, and rarely got to have any time to just see the sights and smell the roses, but at least things rarely fell to shit like they had this morning.

Was this what his life was now? Was he going to be dealing with a constant barrage of annoyances until his dying breath?

Suddenly, being known as "Jin, the djinn who drank too much gin" didn't sound so awful.

No, he couldn't think like that. It was only day one. Yes, *a lot* had happened on day one, but things had to improve. Right?

Fighting to keep his cool, he asked, "Is there anyone else who might be able to swear me in as the new chief of the department?"

"According to the rules here," another officer who was a cyclops, answered, "it has to be someone who holds at least the rank of chief."

Jin sighed.

A new voice came through the speaker. "Sorry to interrupt. This is Rusty, the team's AI. Nice to meet you, sir."

"You, too, Rusty," Jin forced. "Do you know something that may help?"

"Uh, yes. You see, Mistress Kane ranks high enough to swear you in. She's a chief in the technology side of things."

Jin looked up at the cyclops. She held up a finger as her single eye scanned the screen for a few moments. Then she began to nod as she brought her massive eye back up.

Her nodding continued.

"Great. Where is she, Rusty?"

"I'm right here."

Jin turned to locate the face and body that belonged to the sensuous voice that'd just spoken. Just like any succubus, she was radiant, though in a dark sort of way. Black hair, black eyes, high cheekbones, vinyl clothing, and heels that had to have been nearly ten inches. The tails of a whip could be seen flowing down her side. It was clearly attached to her back somehow.

She walked into the room, causing everyone to swoon...men and women alike.

Even Jin's brain felt instantly better at her presence, while at the same time feeling somewhat worse. Differently worse, but worse nonetheless.

"C...ca...uh...ca...uh..."

"Can," she said, helpfully.

"Can you...uh...sw...um..."

"Can I swear you in as the new chief?" she asked, cracking a smile at Jin's obvious distress. "I can." She grabbed the chair next to Jin and spun it around so the back of it faced him. She then straddled the seat and sat down, placing her arms on the top of the seat back. "The question, Jin Kannon, is what's in it for me?"

He was honestly prepared to offer her anything she wanted at that moment. That was partly because his brain was burning, but mostly it was because of who she was.

Knowing he had to get control of the situation—and

fast—Jin reached deep within his psyche and pulled forth as much power as he could from his ink. A hint of magic started to flow through him. It felt like there should've been more, but it was enough to shield himself from the magical allure of a succubus.

He sat up and deadened his eyes. "What's in it for you is having a new chief who isn't going to make your life a living hell."

She smirked. "A challenge. I like that." Reaching a hand up, she snapped her fingers. "Horse boy, get me the book with the swearing-in information."

The officer with long, thick hair jumped from his chair and rushed over to a line of books near the wall. Within seconds he had found what was commanded of him, flipped it open to the page required, and ran over to place it gingerly into the succubus' hand.

"Okay, repeat after me. 'I, Jin Kannon.'" She looked up.

"I, Jin Kannon."

"'Am a naughty boy.'"

"Am a naughty bo…" He frowned at her. "Do it right."

She giggled in a very inappropriate way. "'I, Jin Kannon, hereby swear to uphold the law of the San Diego Paranormal Police Department.'"

Jin repeated it word for word.

"'I will, to the best of my ability, serve, protect, and defend normals against all supernatural activity deemed vile and/or destructive.'"

Again, he said the words.

"'I will protect my team at the cost of my own life, should the need arise.'"

Said that, too.

"'And I will follow all rules, set forth by the Paranormal Police Department, amendable by the Directors of my specific division, so help me science.'"

"…so help me science."

"Okay," she added, after snapping the book shut, "by the power entrusted in me by the Fraternal Order of Paranormal Police Officers, and in accordance with Rule 19 of the PPD Officer Guide, Revision 7, Subsection 23, I, Technology Chief Madison Kane, hereby declare you, Jin Kannon, to be the acting chief of the San Diego Paranormal Police Department." She then held out her hand, showing Jin a ring with an onyx stone. "You may kiss my ring."

He did.

She giggled.

Jin rolled his eyes and sighed, but the pain in his head disappeared almost entirely.

"Funny. Being serious for a moment, I'm the chief now, right?"

Madison Kane got to her feet and handed the book back to the officer who had given it to her. "You're all set, and you're welcome. At some point, you'll need to come visit me and offer a proper thank you."

With that, she turned and sauntered back out of the room.

Jin would've been lying if he said he wasn't thoroughly considering thanking her properly rather soon.

CHAPTER 11

Hector

$\mathcal{H}$ector was proud of his team. They'd not only done what he'd asked of them, they looked rather chuffed about it. Nobody had gotten hurt, including Chief Frannie Fysh. He was most pleased with that fact, truth be told.

"And we didn't even bruise the bitch, did we boys?" said Sofia.

They were all smiles as they shook their heads.

Hector beamed at that. He fully expected grim faces that were filled with disappointment. They liked cracking heads. It was in their blood. But, it seemed, they also quite enjoyed accomplishing a mission to the letter of the commands given them.

That was good. Great, in fact.

If he could run this chapter of the cartel with minimal destruction, Hector would be in his element. Mr. Becerra would tolerate it, too, as long as the money kept coming in and *The San Diego Dogs* remained at the top of the crime syndicate in the area.

Hector firmly believed he could improve their numbers by using non-violent methods. Sometimes violence was necessary. It went with the territory of being a crime boss. Showing a desire to *not* be violent unless there was no alternative, however, would feed deeper into the psyche of the community. He was certain the people would feel less fear and more pride. People would band together and support *The Dogs* in order to avoid greater clashes. That, in turn, would force Mr. Becerra to change his way of thinking, since he was all about family. If Hector could show that people who didn't even directly get paid would support the cartel's efforts in order to avoid violence, the family would grow. It cost nothing but self-control, and the effects were far-reaching.

He just had to prove it.

With a nod toward their prisoner, Sofia pulled off the burlap hood, revealing the beautiful Chief Fysh beneath.

She squinted for a few moments as her eyes adjusted to the light and then furrowed her brow.

"Hector?"

"You remember me. How nice."

"I've known you for three years," she replied. "We dated for months, remember?"

He licked his lips and glanced around nervously. "Did we? I don't know. I have had many girlfriends."

Frannie tilted her head in confusion. "You told me I was your first. You said that you were notably bad with women and then you cried for a little while." She shrugged. "I thought it was kind of pathetic, but also a bit cute. I'd never dated anyone so vulnerable before. It was… different."

"Um…I…"

"I found it odd when you asked me to spank you whenever you were bad, but to each their own. It was a new experience for me, and I like to try everything at least once. I figured maybe you had mommy issues or something."

Hector's crew were shaking their heads at him as he blushed.

"So now what?" Frannie asked. "Did you bring me here to spank me back or is this simply the dull, and stupid, tradition of kidnapping the outgoing chief bit?"

The head of the local cartel thought about that for a second. "Both?"

Frannie shrugged. "Well, at least I'll get something out of it." She glanced around. "Where's your dad? Shouldn't he be running this?"

"Yes, well, my father passed away a while ago and we've been keeping it under wraps."

"Oh, shit." She gave him a consoling look. "You have my sympathies, even if I truly despised the guy."

"Thanks?"

"No problem." Frannie began looking around the room. "It's been a while since the last time I was at one of your houses. Is this the place with the nice pool? I was heading out for a dip at Sea World when your goons abducted me." She gave him a sideways glance. "You know how cranky I get when I've been out of the water for too long."

"You want me to smack the bitch, boss?" asked Sofia,

clearly noticing that Frannie was trying to gain the upper hand.

Hector felt himself growing a bit irritated. Not at Sofia, but rather at Frannie. Her sympathies hadn't seemed very heartfelt at all. Sure, Hector's father had never exactly been nice to Frannie, and it'd been him who insisted that Hector break things off with the PPD chief, but that didn't give her the right to barely express true sympathy for his situation. Worse than that, there was an unwritten rule that said whatever happened between two consenting adults should remain private.

Chief Fysh was playing dirty.

"That won't be necessary, Sofia. However, you may feel free to put her in our driest room. The one that overlooks the pool below."

His command garnered a fierce look from Frannie Fysh.

He puffed out his lips. "Aw, does that make da widdle fishy mad? You have my sympathies." He dropped the little kid act and gave her a disappointed frown instead. "Maybe that will make you think twice before being unkind, not to mention having loose lips when sharing private information, Chief Fysh."

The burlap bag went back over her head and the soldiers started taking her out of the room.

"No more spankings for you, Hector," she cried out. "And if you think I'm ever going to peg you again, you can forget about that, too. Talk about loose lips."

The soldiers stopped abruptly and stared back at him in shock.

He tugged at his collar. "What? I was experimenting."

Fysh stood up straight, though the bag remained on her head. "He's right. That's true. It *was* all experimenting."

"See? Thank you, Frannie. Nothing wrong with a little kindness between—"

"At least the first couple of times," she continued. "Around the twenty-third time of my wearing the 'Rubber Stallion'—as he called it—I'd say it'd moved into desire, at least it seemed that way with all the begging."

"Sheesh, boss, that's pretty intense," Sofia said. "Don't get me wrong. I'm not judging. Cano faces the other way most of the time when we're getting busy."

Cano coughed. "What?"

The other soldiers took a small step away from Cano.

"But, I gotta say, boss, I never pegged you…" Sofia paused. "Sorry, poor choice of words. I mean, I never *considered* you to be the type who had one of those 'deliveries in the rear' tattoos."

Cano tucked the back of his shirt into his trousers.

"Oh, Hector doesn't have one of those," Frannie said.

"See?" Hector sighed.

"I am amazed he's not bald on the back of his head, though. He was always yelling, 'Pull my hair and call me names!'" The burlap sack moved back and forth. "Again, I'm all for trying things, but after a few months of that I was starting to lose interest."

"A few months?" scoffed Cano. "That's pretty crazy." He glanced around at the others. "Am I right or am I right?"

"It's been nearly a year with you, Cano," Sofia said in Hector's defense.

The soldiers took another step away.

Cano held out his hands and imploringly said, "Babe, please!"

"Heh," laughed Frannie. "That's the same thing Hector used to cry out when my rubber buddy smacked his lower back."

"What the hell?" Hector's face filled with rage. "Get that pain in my ass...um...I mean, just get her out of here, already!"

CHAPTER 12

Jin

 With his brain back to normal, Jin was finally able to get a full grip of the situation. Chief Frannie Fysh, who was also supposed to be his new boss, had been kidnapped. Admittedly, that wasn't great, but it fit the motif of the rest of the day.

"All right," he said, getting to his feet and looking out at the sea of faces, "now that I'm able to function as a human being again, why don't I explain a little about myself and then you guys can all do the same for me?"

They all nodded in response, after first giving each other looks. Jin may not have been a top-notch detective just yet, and probably wouldn't be for quite some time, but something was definitely awry.

He chewed his lip for a second. "You've already researched me, haven't you?"

They nodded again.

He should've expected that. Who wouldn't want to

know about the new guy coming in to run the show? He would. The more intel you had, the better your chances of playing your cards right.

It was smart, actually. Hell, Jin did the same thing when researching targets.

That thought shot into his head and right back out again, fast. Did that mean he had more access to his past self on a subconscious level? It would make sense. Even if integration scrambled his noggin pretty solidly, that didn't mean everything was completely gone. It was more like someone had given him thousands of tiny puzzle pieces, most of which were devoid of any color, and didn't even bother to show him a picture of what he was expected to build.

"Okay, obviously you know about my past. But you should also know I've been through a full integration process, which effectively means each of you probably has more information about my past than I do." He knelt down and picked up his hat, putting it back on. For some reason, he just felt more comfortable wearing the damn thing. "It's all fuzzy to me. There are moments when I get a hint of clarity, but for the most part, it's just a blur." He sighed. "Probably for the best, honestly, seeing that this is supposed to be a new start."

The guy who had gotten the book for Mistress...*Miss* Kane raised his hand.

"Yes?"

"Did you really assassinate one thousand people?" The way he asked it was almost as if he'd found it fascinating.

"That's what they tell me," Jin replied. "Your name?"

"Lieutenant Cornell. Clive Cornell. You can just call me Clive if you want."

"Ever killed anyone in the line of duty, Clive?"

Clive looked suddenly put upon.

Jin couldn't blame him. In his current frame of mind, taking a life, even in the line of duty, wasn't exactly a pleasant thought. He frowned, hoping it'd *never* been a pleasant thought, even if it was what he'd done for a living. Had it been, though?

He remembered the last kill and he had to admit it hadn't exactly sucked to remove Hinkers from the face of the world. That asshole had brought nothing but pain and torment, as far as Jin could tell.

"More times than I can count," Clive replied finally.

"Did you enjoy it?"

"No! I was just doing what I had to do in order to protect the public."

"Good." Jin swept his eyes over everyone else. "I'm a different person than I was yesterday. I know that sounds suspect, but each of you has had to go through integration and reintegration since being topside." They all shuddered. "Yeah, you know what it does to you."

Jin sure as hell knew. One thing he was confident of was that he'd never been just some mindless killer. Looking at his new crew made him think it'd be wise to be sure they understood that fact.

"I could easily just say I was doing my job, too—as an assassin, I mean. It would be true. But mine was obviously not a normal job. As a cop, you sometimes have to pull the trigger to protect the innocent. Believe it or not, the same goes for an assassin, assuming that assassin only takes contracts for people who are seriously awful." He took his hat off again and sat it on the little table next to him. "It all started when I was pretty young. I had the skills, the magic, the vinegar, and a very poor childhood. Both my parents died when I was eleven years old, having been caught in the middle of a firefight between two rival crime lords in the Badlands." He swallowed hard, still recalling their lifeless eyes. "A lady appeared on the scene and wiped out everyone within seconds. She was an assassin. She saw me and took pity."

It seemed Jin was able to recall a lot of that part of his life. He wasn't sure why that was, or why he was diving into this story with this team at all. It seemed somewhat counterintuitive, but his brain was pushing him to keep going. Was it part of the integration process that was somehow still lingering? Probably. Whatever. It was better than sitting naked in the center of a room on a chair covered with plastic that he'd ultimately soil.

Then again, maybe not.

"I was with her until the age of nineteen when she was gunned down by one of the rival assassins who worked for the crime lords."

The memory haunted Jin to this day. Effectively, it was like having yet another parent killed.

"I wasn't happy," he rasped. "I remember staring down at her in horror and then looking back up at the shit-eating grin of the guy who'd just taken her life." He could feel his eyes start to burn. "Something in me snapped and my ink flared up, driving power through me. One moment I was standing next to the body of the woman who had helped raise me after my parents died. The next moment I was standing behind the guy who had killed her as his body fell straight forward, a knife handle sticking out from the back of his skull."

That's when Jin noticed everyone was leaning a little away from him, fear etched on their faces.

"My eyes are glowing, aren't they?"

"Yeah, chief," answered the leprechaun, "and they're after lookin' freaky as fuck."

"Sorry. When I get riled up, that happens. They'll cool off in a minute." Jin inclined his head toward her. "Your name?"

"Lacy Meany. I'm a Lieutenant, too. I'm also a leprechaun. And before ye ask, since everyone usually does…yes, I'm after bein' magically delicious."

"Okay, that's…" Jin wouldn't have asked her that question, and it was surprising anyone ever did. "Well, it's nice to meet you, Lacy."

He closed his eyes and focused on calming down just enough to cool off his eyes. They'd continue to glow for a bit, but slow breathing tended to make them dim more quickly.

"The point, guys, is that it wasn't like I'd set out to be an assassin. I kind of fell into it, and I was clearly quite good at it, even if I can't remember the majority of the kills." He tried digging into his memory again, but each image that flashed was quickly replaced by a blank space. "The one thing I know for certain is that I never took a contract for a target who wasn't a seriously bad person. That was my rule. I wanted to stop the bad people from doing to other kids what they'd done to me."

"Altruistic Assassin, then." That was the cyclops. She

quickly added, "Sergeant Chimichanga, but everyone calls me Chimi. I'm a seer."

"Always good to have a seer around," Jin said. The rest of the room shook their heads, though Chimi hadn't seen that. He got the feeling he shouldn't ask why they didn't consider it a good thing.

Instead, he turned toward the other guy in the room, the one with reddish-black hair. "And you are?"

"Captain Rudy Valdez...or just Rudy. I'm a wererooster."

That admission caught Jin off guard. He'd never heard of such a thing before, which got him thinking about the rest of the crew. There was a leprechaun, a wererooster, a cyclops, a unicorn, and a succubus for a chief technician.

He looked at Clive. "What—"

"Centaur." Clive held up a hand. "Yeah, I know I don't look like one. I ended up with mostly the human parts of both parents. It's kind of embarrassing if I'm being honest, but I'm a solid cop and I have some special skills that I *did* get from my folks."

Nobody said anything for about ten seconds, and then Lacy blurted, "He can neigh so loud as ta make ye crap yer britches."

"He also has a magic tail that does all sorts of tricks," noted Chimi.

Rudy leaned forward. "He can also shit while he's walking along. Like it's nothing, too. Just walking and next thing you know there's shit flopping out."

"Dude!"

"What?" Rudy's hands were up. "You do it all the time."

"I do not!" Clive was blushing. "It's been nearly a year since I've done that, you tiny-dicked chicken-fucker."

Rudy raised an eyebrow. "What's wrong with being a chicken-fucker?"

"Well, I mean, when you're in rooster form, nothing. It's when you're not that it's—"

"RIGHT!" Jin called out quickly. "Well, now that we know the basics about each other, and some unfortunately not-so-basics, we should probably focus our attention on finding Chief Fysh, eh?"

Nobody argued, though Rudy thankfully hissed over, "You know I don't do that when in human form, Mr. Ed."

"And you know I don't shit-walk anymore, cock-gobbler."

Those two were obviously going to be "fun" to manage.

While Jin had the sudden urge to turn around and walk into his new office, it just didn't feel right. Yes, he'd been officially sworn into the position, but only because his head had been on the verge of exploding. Before *actually* taking the full reins, Jin wanted it to be done right. That's not to say he wasn't going to do his damnedest to lead the team until such time that Chief Fysh could be liberated from her current position, shake his hand, hand him the keys to the team, and then head off to her new Director position on the force.

Right now, though, it just didn't seem right.

In other words, Jin's name wasn't on the door yet. Chief Fysh's was, and it was going to stay that way until everything was made official.

"You all know your positions better than I do, and you

certainly know this town better than me. So I'm not about to start doling out orders. If anything, I need to lean on you guys until I get my feet on the ground." He looked over at Raina. "You're apparently my new deputy, so I'll rely on you most."

"Of course, sir. Happy to help!"

"Jin," he corrected her.

"You want some gin?" she replied, looking confused. "It's barely past noon, sir, and if I may say—"

"I meant that you should call me Jin," he interrupted with a smile, though gin honestly didn't sound all that bad at the moment.

"Ah! Right. Sorry, sir." She coughed lightly. "I mean, Jin." It was said somewhat uncomfortably.

"Something wrong?"

"If it's all the same to you, sir, I'd rather keep calling you 'sir,' sir. Or chief, if that's okay."

Another glance around the room told him they all preferred that level of protocol.

Maybe that wasn't such a bad thing when he thought about it. Jin was the new chief, so it could be that starting off with a bit more formality was the wise thing to do, at least for now. In time, that may change, possibly when we're off-duty.

"Whatever you feel most comfortable with is fine by me." He held up a finger. "By the way, nobody actually calls Miss Kane by the name 'Mistress Kane,' right?"

"Only Rusty," answered Rudy. "He's got a thing for her."

Jin was perplexed at how that could be but shook the feeling away. He didn't understand enough about computers and artificial intelligence to know if it was normal or not. Seemed like it wasn't, but who was he to judge?

Hell, ever since getting this damned PPD tattoo on his arm, he'd felt more amorous than he'd ever felt, and seeing Mistress—dammit—*Miss* Kane certainly had his engines revving more than usual.

"Okay, well, unless anyone disagrees, I'd say it'd be a smart move to split up and start searching. Yes?"

Nobody answered, they all just got up and started heading for the door.

Jin followed, hearing Rudy whisper to Clive, "So our new chief is Jin the djinn who likes to drink gin?"

They giggled as Jin's shoulders slumped ever so slightly.

CHAPTER 13

Vestin

*I*t was all playing out better than expected. The new head of the local cartel was weak compared to his deceased father. That would not bode well for the destiny of San Diego. Once it fell under the new rule of Vestin DeLanté, he would set his eyes up the coast of California. Soon, he would completely control the West. That would prove his plan was solid, and then he would move across the country while simultaneously combing through Europe.

For now, he would remain patient. Fortunately, patience was something vampires were well equipped to manage.

Vestin's general, Prender, walked into the room and took a knee before the throne.

Yes, Vestin had a throne, just as any vampiric commander should. It was necessary when it came to true nobility. It represented status, yes, but more importantly, it prompted a chain of command that those of pure blood took seriously.

"We exhumed the body as you commanded, My Lord."

"And?"

The man kept his head bowed, not breaking protocol in the least. "The previous leader of the cartel reanimated as expected."

"His words?"

"No, sir. Those are my words."

Vestin fought to keep from sighing. "I'm asking what Emiliano said when you dug him up, Prender."

"Ah, right. Sorry, My Lord. He said, 'I shall stand and serve Lord Vestin,' just as you anticipated."

"Excellent."

And it *was* excellent. It proved that Vestin's work had not been wasted. His peers in the Netherworld had always chided him when he spoke of his ambitions. They called him foolish, but he knew it could be done.

For thousands of years, vampires had been capable of possessing the bodies and minds of normals. It was a forbidden practice topside, though many still maintained a healthy stable of slaves. That's why the missing persons boards in most normal police precincts were filled these days. Some of the nobility in the Netherworld had even been brazen enough to smuggle normals down to serve them in the dark shadows without the supernatural police knowing about it. But the one thing that'd always been out of reach for vampires was the ability to control the minds and bodies of other supers unless said supers allowed it due to taking medications that lowered their natural immunity, of course. Sadly, those people were few and far between. It could also be done with witches, warlocks, and certain types of slugs, though nobody ever wanted to engage in that practice anymore. It was too slimy.

In other words, in general, supers of all types had grown a natural immunity when it came to vampire bites.

Until now.

Through Vestin's work with chemistry, biology, artificial intelligence, and magic, he'd been able to adjust his DNA to make his venom capable of dominating the blood of supers, bypassing their immune systems entirely.

He'd attempted it on a few guards from *The San Diego Dogs* about eight months back, and it'd worked, though it'd admittedly taken longer than expected to perfect. After numerous tweaks, however, he'd proven it could work on demand. That's when he set out to attempt it on one of their toughest.

His target had been Emiliano, the alpha of *The Dogs* pack. The man had run the cartel for years and he was a ruthless boss. He tolerated no dissension in the ranks. His mind was tough, his body was tough, and he certainly had an above-average immune system.

Vestin believed if his bite could tame the likes of Emiliano, his venom could rule the world.

His belief appeared to have been correct.

"Where is he?"

Prender got to his feet and turned to the side, snapping his fingers. In response, the hulking Emiliano—

or at least the zombified version of him—slowly entered the room. His face had already begun the process of deterioration and he was dragging his left foot with each step, but it was definitely Emiliano. It did look as though he'd partially morphed into his wolf form, however. His claws were hanging out of his hands, anyway.

Stopping ten feet back, the zombie lowered his head slightly, proving he had indeed become the slave of Vestin. There was no way a man like Emiliano would've bowed to anyone in the past.

"Who do you serve?" Vestin asked, just to be sure.

"Vestin," came a rasp that contained a bit of a gurgle.

It wasn't a pleasant sound.

The odor that wafted like a thick cloud of unfortunate fumes finally touched Vestin's nasal passages as well. He brought his kerchief to his nose as his eyes began to water.

Nonetheless, Vestin had what he needed to set his full plan in motion, and he couldn't wait to prove to the fools who doubted him how wrong they'd been. Once he had taken complete control of the world topside, he would turn his attention to the Netherworld, first striking the Badlands before tearing down the wall between the two lands. Once Netherworld Proper was under his command, the Vestian Empire would be complete.

Then who would be the fool?

Vestin leaned forward slightly. "You will become the driving force of my slave kingdom topside Emiliano. Do you understand?"

"I understand."

He wanted to turn the screws a little, though he wasn't

sure if it would even bother someone like Emiliano, especially in his current state.

"Your son has taken over your position as head of *The San Diego Dogs*, you know?"

There was indeed a groan.

That pleased Vestin.

"To be fair to your son, the PPD is getting a new chief and Hector has successfully upheld the tradition of kidnapping the old one." He scratched the armrest lightly. "Though I do believe he used to date her, no?"

Another groan.

"Yes, children can be so trying, can they not?" He hadn't bothered to wait for an answer. "Personally, I think having your son managing the cartel here is going to be rather useful to us. He's weak. He wants to be 'good' to the community. He wants them included in everything, minimizing violence wherever possible."

"Sickening," said Emiliano. "I sometimes wonder if he's truly from my loins."

Vestin grinned. "Worry not, Emiliano, for when the time comes, Hector will fall in line just like everyone else. Nobody is beyond my reach, not even the great Emiliano, yes?"

"Yes."

"Yes, indeed. Prender, have the slaves clean Emiliano up as they've done with each other. I believe the time has come to begin rolling out *Shade*."

"*Shade*, My Lord?"

"You don't like it, Prender?"

"Oh, uh, I mean…well…" He tugged at his collar. "I've

never been one for naming things, but I'm sure it's just fine, My Lord."

"Hmmm." Vestin was not satisfied with being merely "fine." He sighed. "I considered going with *Darkness* or *Shadow*, but those have both been overused in recent years, you know?"

"As you say, My Lord."

Vestin rolled his eyes. "What do you think, Emiliano?"

"*Shade* sounds weak."

Yes, it did, didn't it? Speaking of weak, Vestin had allowed Emiliano to avoid titles up until now, but that needed to change.

He looked sternly at the zombie and said, "My Lord."

"Yes?"

"No," Vestin stated with a grunt, "*you* shall address *me* as 'My Lord' going forward."

"*Shade* sounds weak, My Lord."

One of the trickiest things any supervillain faced was the naming of their vile creations. Most of the good names had been snapped up long before, and it was impossible to get a decent URL for anything these days, especially since registering a domain at this point only costs ten dollars.

"Do either of you have any ideas for something better?"

The two men looked at each other.

"Again, My Lord, it's not exactly a strength of mine," said Prender.

"Same with me…My Lord."

Vestin frowned at them both.

Truth be told, neither of them would come up with

anything better than *Shade*, anyway, unless they looked in a thesaurus, and he truly doubted they even knew to think of doing such a thing. If they had managed to figure that out, though, they'd not check the name against history, which would result in nothing but a repeat of a past moniker.

That wasn't to say that *Shade* hadn't been used for something in the past, but it certainly wasn't common… probably because it *did*, in fact, sound somewhat weak.

"How about *Nefarium*?" he asked as the idea hit him.

"Not even sure what that means, My Lord."

Emiliano appeared equally perplexed, and that was a strange look on a zombie.

Vestin sighed yet again. "Fine, I'll think of something on my own then. Go about your duties and begin your preparations. I wish to begin bringing…oooh… *Gloominess*?" They shook their heads. "Blast."

"If I may make a suggestion…um…My Lord," Emiliano spoke up, "you might consider hiring a marketing firm. When *The Dogs* started having a drop in drug sales, I hired *Turner, Turner, and Smith*. They helped us turn the ship around."

"Oh?"

"We worked with Janet Smith, specifically. She was less pompous than Turner or Turner, though she's still pretty terrible to work with." He cleared his throat, which sounded rather disgusting in his desiccated state. "Still, she came up with great names for our drugs, like Joy Juice…"

"Interesting."

"…Love Squirt…"

"Moderately perverse."

"…and Orgasmic Spooge Butter."

"Definitely perverse."

"Ultimately," continued Emiliano, "I asked her to aim for something a little less sexual, even though she insisted that sex sells."

"That's been my experience," Prender stated. "My OnlyFans page made me nearly one hundred thousand dollars before Lord Vestin made me shut it down, citing it unbefitting for a man in his army to prance around in thongs for money."

Prender must've realized he'd spoken out of turn because he quickly lowered his head again.

"Anyway," Emiliano went on, "she finally hooked us up with the name Happy Product #7."

For whatever reason, that name caught Vestin's attention. It was vague, yet appealing. It carried with it a mystic allure. You couldn't help but wonder what it was about the product that made you happy, for instance. And why #7? Was that because they'd tried six iterations and had finally landed on the secret sauce? Surely multiple iterations of a product implied a lot of thought, testing, and work had gone into it.

"What was this name a replacement for?" asked Vestin.

"Heroin."

"Ah."

"Sales quadrupled over the next thirty days, and the residuals on that stuff are amazing…My Lord."

Vestin was nodding vigorously. "Yes, yes. I'm sure they are. I will contact these people, as you say. It's a fine plan."

"Thank you, My Lord." They both began to leave the

room when Emiliano stopped and looked slightly over his shoulder. "Note, My Lord, that Janet Smith will require that you sign a DNBA in order to work with her."

"You mean an NDA? A Non-Disclosure Agreement?"

"No, My Lord, a DNBA. It's a Do Not Bite Agreement."

"Ah. Right."

CHAPTER 14

Rudy

*R*udy and Clive sat in the centaur's Mazda Miata convertible. It was the zircon sand metallic one with the black leather interior. Kind of sporty for a guy like Clive.

It fit Rudy perfectly, but he couldn't afford a car these days, at least not for a while. He'd lost too many cockfights over the last two years. Ever since they started using steroids on his competitors, Rudy could barely get a peck in, and he had zero chance whenever the rooster across the ring got a bout of roid rage. Up until then, he'd been the hands-down favorite. Everyone bet on him. Ultimately, though, without even bothering to make a formal announcement, he'd hung up his pecker—in a manner of speaking—and retired.

That would've been fine had he not built a somewhat lavish lifestyle over his years on top. After declaring bankruptcy, losing his house and three cars, and finding himself forced to repay a few debts the courts wouldn't clear, he'd ended up living in a cramped studio apartment near the bus station.

Thankfully, Clive picked him up most nights since they were partners. He was even more thankful that Clive had never said a word about any of it.

Clive was a true pal.

"What do you think of the new chief so far?"

Gripping the wheel a little firmer, Clive said, "Dude, I don't know. On the one hand, he seems like a decent enough guy; on the other, he *was* an assassin and a damn good one at that." They turned right at the light. "I'd be lying if I said I wasn't impressed by the fact that he's got one thousand confirmed kills under his belt."

"It's a pretty crazy number."

"Yeah."

"It's also pretty crazy they just let a guy like him topside and put him in charge of our squad."

"Exactly." Clive pointed over at Rudy. "That's what's bugging me about it."

A car honked at them.

"Eyes on the road, ya floppy penis," complained Rudy.

"Sorry."

"Anyway, it's not that I don't *want* to like the dude," Rudy went on, "it's just that I don't want anyone on the squad to end up as kill one thousand and one."

"Unlikely, but I hear you."

They sat in silence for a few minutes as Clive continued toward one of the "unknown restaurants" off the beaten path. It was a place that had no name and served only certain customers, most notably members of the cartel whenever the boss was in the mood to eat something fancy.

Kidnapping the chief was an honored tradition amongst cartel members, which meant it was celebration time.

"Then again," Clive said, interrupting Rudy's thoughts, "Chief Kannon was right about integrations. They suck, sure, but they're quite effective."

It was hard to argue. It usually took weeks after going through reintegration before Rudy could stand morphing into his rooster form. He was still capable of doing it, and he often had to force it since it tended to play a useful role in his position as a cop, but it wasn't much fun. Hell, he was about to go through the process of morphing and he wasn't a fan at all, and his last reintegration was nearly nine months ago.

"You'd think they'd dig deep into the skull of a guy like that, too."

"*Very* deep," agreed Clive. "I'd be surprised if they didn't get to his brain by way of his asshole if I'm being honest."

Rudy chuckled at that. "Feels like they do even with guys like us."

"No shit."

He wanted to believe Kannon was all clear, but he was struggling. It probably had to do with Rudy being a chicken. They didn't trust many things and with good reason.

Still...

"I don't know, man." Rudy shook his head as they turned the corner and pulled into an area that kept the car well hidden. "It's not like we have much of a choice but to accept it, you know? He's the new chief. We're just peons. If we screw up, he kills us, and that's that."

Clive kept moving the car back and forth until he got it just so. Then he stopped and clicked off the engine.

"I think we're probably both being a bit over-the-top about this dude." He turned slightly in his seat. "He's not going to kill us unless he's got a contract on us, for one. Secondly, he claims to only kill targets who are actually bad people."

"Claims."

"And we're *not* bad people."

"Depends on his definition of bad, dude."

Clive gave him a look. "I think we're both being ridiculous, and it's weird that *I'm* the one bringing that up. You're usually the voice of reason in this partnership."

"Since when?"

Suddenly, Clive's head snapped up and he said, "Ahhh…I see what's going on."

"What?"

"You're about to go full rooster and put yourself in with a bunch of other roosters and chickens."

"Yeah?"

"Come on, ya ball-hair fanatic, you always get dramatic when that happens."

"Your mom gets dramatic when that happens."

Clive grinned. "See?"

Rudy slumped forward. "Okay, fine, so I don't want to do this. But if I don't, you know what's going to happen?"

"The new chief will find out and shoot you?" Clive was clearly being sardonic. "Let's be fair, though, man…

wouldn't any chief?" He started to do a poor impersonation of Chief Kannon, moving his hands around and getting all animated. "What do you mean Captain Valdez refused to turn into a rooster? I have wasted the worst of the worst in the Badlands, but in all my years I've never heard of anything so disturbing as this! Guess I'll have to assassinate that bad chicken!"

In response, Rudy slumped even further, recognizing he was being quite ridiculous. "Well, it sounds stupid when you say it like that."

"Li'l bit."

"And I'm a rooster, *not* a chicken." Rudy drew in a deep breath, hardening his resolve before opening the door and sticking his leg out. "Fuck you, donkey nuts."

"Fuck you, too, feather butt."

They both got out and looked around.

Rudy felt a bit better about what he needed to do. Of all the partners Rudy'd had over the years, only Clive had ever been able to cut to the quick in such a way that didn't make Rudy want to kill him…much.

"You're a dick, Clive," Rudy said, keeping his eyes on the restaurant as they slowly moved toward it. "I mean that with all my heart, too." They stopped at the cage and Rudy started to morph into his rooster form. "Still, I appreciate the pep-talk."

"What are partners for?"

CHAPTER 15

Lacy

*L*acy liked riding along with Chimi. The big oaf drove around on a souped-up scooter, enhanced by Miss Kane to carry the cyclops' weight. It was also a lot faster than the stock version. Plus, it was red. Lacy liked red.

The only part that bugged her was how Chimi refused to start puttering along until Lacy put on a helmet. There was no need for a leprechaun to wear any protection whatsoever. Sure, she could get crushed, shot, kicked—that happened more when she was younger—and all that, but she effectively floated along anyway, so even if there was a crash Lacy would most certainly not be injured.

Still, it was admittedly sweet that Chimi cared enough about her, so Lacy always obliged.

They pulled up to Ocean Beach, also known as "Hippie Beach," and Chimi put a large lock in place to secure the scooter. That, too, was not necessary. Everyone in the area was so laid back, they wouldn't bother swiping her scooter. And even if they tried, they'd be incapable of getting it to start. Kane had rigged it to only work in conjunction with a PPD tattoo.

Again, though, that was Chimi for you. She had a set way of doing things, and there was little chance you could budge her on anything.

It was borderline OCD.

While Chimi went through her security ritual, Lacy took off her helmet and snapped her fingers, causing it to shrink down and disappear into her pack.

"I'm after liking the new chief," she said. "Doesn't seem like a mindless killer to me."

"My readings on him were clear."

"Which is the only thing that has me worried," Lacy replied, her eyes roving around the area as she sought out their normal informants.

"Why?"

That's when Lacy realized she'd said her piece aloud.

"No reason."

Everyone on the force knew that Chimi's readings were 99% inaccurate. If she said to go north, you went south. If she said to shoot high, you shot low. If she said to use silver breaker bullets, you used wood. Actually, these days you just use the new style of breaker bullets developed by the tech guy from the Las Vegas PPD. Those breakers contained all sorts of junk to waste just about any super without having to think first. Anyway, even though Lacy thought Chimi's astrological bullshit was, well, bullshit, she had to admit that for the cyclops to be so consistently wrong lent credence to the fact that she was just bad at reading what was otherwise 99% accurate.

The point regarding Chief Kannon being one of the world's greatest thinkers was certainly incorrect, but Lacy was more concerned about the part where Chimi's cards said he was mostly harmless.

A lifelong assassin who was no longer an enormous threat *could* be constructed from the integration process, but there was no way it'd hold forever. Hell, even Lacy's magic had a shelf life. She could cast her best enchantments on a beautiful flower, pushing to give it a long life, but eventually, it'd fade away. Integration was like that, except that Lacy's magic was much stronger.

Too bad she couldn't use it in a way to make sure the new chief kept his cool.

Bah. That was dumb. The guy was fine. There was no way he'd have been allowed topside if he was still that much of a threat.

Chimi finished her security checks and nodded at Lacy.

"All set."

"Except yer helmet, ya big doof."

"Oh, oops."

That happened almost every time, which Lacy found funny. Chimi was rigorous with her inspections, except when it came to her helmet. She always forgot about it.

About a minute later, they were ready to go.

"I like the new chief," Chimi said while they walked along. "He's real if you know what I mean?"

Lacy knew exactly what she meant. Coming from Chimi, though, it was an odd statement. While Chimi was super friendly and caring, she wasn't exactly the best at reading people. But in this case, Lacy couldn't argue with her.

"I do, actually," Lacy said. "That's what's been after buggin' me. He's supposed ta be some kinda mass killer, aye? But he's…likable."

"He's not a mass killer, Lacy. He was an assassin and he'd done it for a very long time." Chimi stopped and picked up a candy bar wrapper from the ground. She threw it into the nearest basket. "It's not like he shot one thousand people over the course of a month or anything."

"Fair point." Lacy was confused at the level of acumen Chimi appeared to have when it came to Chief Kannon. "Though ye'd have to admit he's certainly killed loads more than just those he'd been after targetin'."

"I suppose that's true. My instincts tell me that even those people were very bad, though."

"Aye, I suppose that makes sense."

And it did, making Lacy feel better about Chimi's perspective. She'd used logic. Logic made sense. Throwing wads of peanut butter against a brick wall and seeing how long it took to fall to the ground in order to make predictions was *not* logical. Not that Chimi'd ever done that, but the things she *did* do were equally batty to someone like Lacy…and Lacy was a frickin' leprechaun!

They stopped at the edge of the bridge.

The informants the PPD usually went after were a couple of local supers. Their names were Petey and Raffy.

Petey was a "fallen angel," meaning he was the result of a one-night stand between a demon and a pixie who neglected to use protection. That made him an outcast of sorts. Pixies relentlessly taunted him because he wasn't pure; demons shunned him because he was part pixie. He wasn't the best with insults, like most pixies, and he couldn't possess larger creatures like most demons. As a result, Petey had spent most of his time drinking, getting stoned, and possessing garden gnomes. Fortunately, his best friend was Raffy, who was about the only other dude in the world Petey could be himself around.

That's because Raffy was a bigfoot who wore Hawaiian shirts, cargo shorts, and magically-modified sunglasses. Come to think of it, all his clothes had been magically enhanced in order to fit him. While the supers knew he was a bigfoot—though they all called him a stinkfoot because the smell of his feet could melt titanium —normals just thought he was a big, hairy dude. He, too, drank a lot and got stoned all the time.

Raffy and Petey were pals, through and through, and even though they were both pretty consistently baked, they had a way of knowing things about the area that even the PPD had difficulty figuring out.

"See them anywhere?" asked Chimi.

"Nah. Guessin' they're through the zone."

"Yep."

Ugh.

Ocean Beach was nice enough, even to someone like Lacy who preferred avoiding the ocean. There were a number of tourists, mostly normals, who visited the place, and a lot of hippies, almost always normals, who hung around pretty much all the time. Most of them smelled pretty rough, causing her to cast "Vanilla" on her own nose whenever she first caught wind of one. None of them could hold a candle to Raffy, at least not without causing a fire, but collectively they could at least melt a refrigerated stick of butter.

Generally, normals stopped at a certain point on the beach, keeping their distance as if there was some kind of hidden barrier in place.

There was.

It was known as a null zone, which was coupled with a hidden zone. The null zone part gave normals an eerie feeling that made them steer clear of an area. The hidden zone aspect was a magical facade where normals merely saw the extension of the beach. Supers, however, could see what was truly on the other side of the "wall."

In this instance, what Lacy saw were a bunch of supernaturals playing volleyball, sunbathing, and basically just having a nice day.

Raffy and Petey were a little further down, staying back near the cliff face with their backs against the rocks. They were hitting the bong like it was an oxygen tank. She'd often wondered how they managed such a lifestyle after dealing with reintegration. The only thing she could think of was the brand of "weed" they smoked up here. It was your standard pot but laced with hippie magic.

Lacy doubled her vanilla-scent magic immediately when they got close enough. As for Chimi, she breathed in deeply and let out a satisfied moan.

Chimi was a strange one.

"Sup, dudes?" asked Raffy, after releasing a massive gust of weed smoke.

"That stuff isn't good for you," Chimi said. "Burns your brain cells."

"That's why we do it," replied Petey before his eyes got big and bright. That always happened when he saw Lacey. In a flash, he sprouted wings and flew up to her. "Hello, my love."

"Back off, before I cast a spell on ya that'll be after makin' yer weed do nothin' of use!"

Petey moved his hands to cover his privates. "You wouldn't."

Lacy frowned. "I'm talkin' about the weed yer smokin', ye daft angel."

Flying back down, Petey stood protectively in front of the bong. "That's even worse!"

"Bah!"

As for Chimi, she'd gotten too close to Raffy again. That was obvious because her demeanor changed instantly. She was currently twirling her hair and moving her foot around in the sand.

"Hey, Raffy," she said, but was acting like she was chewing gum. She wasn't chewing gum. "You know I didn't mean that thing I said about you smoking. I think it makes you sexy."

Lacy rolled her eyes.

"Peace, man," Raffy replied, clearly oblivious to how Chimi felt.

At least Lacy knew how Petey felt about her. She thought he was cute, too, except when he was possessing a gnome or being incredibly needy.

She snapped her fingers in front of Chimi's face.

"Earth to Chimi. Come innnnnn, Chimi."

Chimi blinked a few times, which looked pretty weird over that big eye, and then took a step back.

"I did it again, didn't I?"

"Ye did, aye." Lacy patted her on the shoulder. "His pheromones must be stronger than usual, I'm after guessin'. Usually ye ain't all giddy unless yer downwind and we ain't downwind." She began moving her hands around. "Me thinks ye'll be needin' this."

A thin stream of light left Lacy's fingers and surrounded Chimi's nostrils.

Chimi choked for a few seconds, wiping at her face as the magic took full hold of her. Finally, she stopped and her eye cleared up completely.

"Thank you," she whispered before turning back to Raffy. "We have questions."

He seemed clueless about what'd just happened. "All right, man."

Petey slumped down onto his little tattered towel and grunted. "It's the only time you come to see us."

"Why else would we come to see you?" asked Chimi. "You're informants, right?"

"Sure. Yeah. Nothing more than that. Just crappy, inconsequential informants."

It was Lacy's turn to groan.

She knew what he was doing. He was moping because they'd shared a fling before he'd turned into a hippie. It'd been nothing serious...from her side. Petey, however, had launched into full boyfriend mode, trying to make an enduring relationship that was based on "love, romance, and the respect of two individuals who want more in their lives than physical trysts." Those were his words, and Lacy didn't share in the sentiment. She never wanted to be tied down, except for pleasure and even that was rare.

She'd been totally upfront about her relationship avoidance with Petey *before* they'd boned. Again, though, Lacy was magically delicious.

One bite of the proverbial fruit and he couldn't resist wanting more.

She should've known better, especially since it'd happened nearly every time she hopped in the sack with someone.

The entire thing kind of made her feel bad, wishing she'd never gotten involved with him in the first place. He craved love; she craved freedom. That's not a good mix.

Chimi, who'd regained herself since receiving a solid magical shield to ward off Raffy's scent, wasn't great with sarcasm. "Exactly, Petey. We have questions and you're informants. I wouldn't say you're crappy ones, though. Your information is usually pretty good."

Raffy clearly saw his buddy's plight and said, "What do you want, man?"

"The chief has been kidnapped."

"Yeah, so?"

"Do you know where she is?"

Petey crossed his arms. "Obviously with the cartel."

"Aye, obviously," Lacy agreed, turning a bit sour. She couldn't help it. He was blaming her for everything…still. "The cartel's not a tiny widget now, though, is it? What she's after askin' is where the blast they're housin' the chief, and ye know it. Yer just being cantankerous cause ye ain't listened when I told ye I wasn't gonna play the role of girlfriend to anybody."

There were a few moments of silence after that explosion.

"Main house, man," Raffy replied. "Hector's been…like, you know, camping there or something since his daddy, well, like…started feeding the trees, man."

Lacy and Chimi glanced at each other, clearly confused by that statement.

"What's that mean?" asked Chimi.

The two stoners shared a look that time. Actually, only Raffy was a genuine pothead. Weed and booze on Petey lasted only 20-30 seconds. It was another side effect of being a fallen angel.

"Wait," said Petey, changing his annoyed expression into one that represented incredulousness, "the PPD didn't know Emiliano died?" The two cops shook their heads in unison. "Wow. That's kind of lame. I mean, I get it when you need to find out some hidden information and so you come down here to ask for the inside scoop. But we're talking about the *head* of the cartel, which has to make up ninety percent or more of your work."

He wasn't wrong. It *was* embarrassing. The cartels were great at hiding information, though. Something this big shouldn't have made it through, obviously, but at the same time something this big would be put under the tightest security clearance. It made her wonder how these two idiots were able to know what they knew.

She wasn't going to broach that subject. It wouldn't be worth it. They'd never tell, and when she really thought about it she didn't want to know anyway. While they may have had a tumultuous relationship, the cops needed the information. If these guys shut their mouths due to being pressured into revealing sources that could well cause their personal extinction, nobody would win...except the cartel, of course.

"I get it," Lacy said. "Hector's after provin' himself and Chief Fysh was walkin' out the door. Tradition and timin'."

"You got it, man," said Raffy.

"Thanks." She tugged on Chimi's sleeve. "Let's go. We've got what we were needin'."

Chimi seemed unsure, but Lacy knew the cyclops respected the hierarchy between them. Lacy was the senior partner. If she said it was time to go, it was time to go.

Besides, she didn't want to have any more arguments with Petey.

Too bad the fallen angel felt differently. "Bye! Thanks for stopping over! Was great to see you, too! Don't forget to write!"

Lacy groaned but kept flying.

CHAPTER 16

Jin

It was very strange to be driving down the road in a modest car of a make and model he'd never heard of, seated next to a person who was apparently a unicorn, while staring out at the ocean as he went on a search for the person he was replacing in a job he probably should never have been given.

But here he was, and he wasn't going to complain about it.

Anymore.

Maybe.

Okay, he probably would but he was certainly going to try not to.

The crisp smell of the air was amazing. It could've just smelled great to Jin, being that he was new around town, but he was fine with that. The places he'd frequented all his life had been dank and often boiling hot. They were dismal, ripe with decay, and often stagnant when it came to airflow. There was a breeze here, even when the car wasn't moving. Plus, the air carried a scent of the sea. It was peaceful, regardless of the haywire world he'd gotten himself into.

"You're not going to kill any of us if we mess up, right?" Raina asked out of the blue, causing Jin to look at her as if she was nuts. She gave him a quick glance since they were stopped. "Wrong thing to ask?" She hadn't waited for a response. "Look, I don't think you will, and neither does Chimi, but some of the others are worried."

Sigh.

He'd already addressed it earlier, but apparently his message hadn't gotten through.

"The only way I'm going to kill any of you is if my aim is off, and my aim is never off." At least it wasn't prior to him undergoing integration, but he didn't think it wise to point that out. "The sooner everyone gets it through their heads that I'm here to help us all do our jobs better, the smoother things are going to go. I *was* an assassin. I'm not anymore." Right? "If I can somehow go through the rest of my days without taking another life, I'm all for it."

Raina brightened. "I knew it. They're just being silly."

Hopefully, that's all it was.

Truthfully, Jin had been an assassin for a very long time and he'd been one of the best. He was good at killing. Very good. For a while, early on in his career, he was also a bit of a hothead. He'd wanted revenge against the world, and that ended up getting directed toward people like those who'd killed his parents. About two hundred kills in, though, he started recognizing taking out targets wasn't easing his pain. That's when he decided to focus inward, to start studying the world at large, and to separate himself from the job he was doing.

It hadn't been easy, taking a solid five years of concerted effort, but he'd done it.

Still, integration or not, killing had been a part of him for too many years for it to disappear overnight.

He could only hope the tools they'd used to refactor his brain had been powerful enough to stop that side of his personality in its tracks. If not, there'd be more bodies in his wake before too long. His only true confidence ran the path of knowing they wouldn't be innocent bodies.

"Where are we going again?" Jin asked.

"Sea World."

"Uh-huh."

"Oh, right. Sorry, chief, I keep forgetting you're not from around here." She adjusted in her chair as they continued along the road. "Basically, it's a big theme park where they keep all sorts of aquatic animals, or animals associated with water so that people can enjoy them."

Jin frowned. "You mean like a buffet?"

"Oh, no! Nothing like that. Think of it more like a zoo."

"Ah. Right. Got it."

It was strange to keep wild beasts caged away for the enjoyment of man. Jin wasn't a fan of it. He wasn't going to complain, though. There was little point. People did what they did, no matter what you thought they should do.

Plus, who was he to make decisions for others? If he didn't like something, he could choose not to participate. Blocking someone else's right to engage made no sense unless they were impacting the rights of someone else by whatever they were doing.

The other possibility, obviously, was if a person ended up as a name on a list and he was contracted to kill them.

When he thought of it that way it became obvious blocking someone else's right to do whatever they wanted was actually a pretty common thing.

Jin's main point of contention when it came to zoos, was that animals didn't have the option to choose between captivity and freedom. If he were being honest, he'd have to admit the animals were likely better off in the zoo, being that they were fed, cleaned, protected, and provided with medical services, but they may not have felt that way.

They pulled into the park and drove along a little road Jin knew the normals couldn't see. It wouldn't even have looked strange to any of them to find a car had simply disappeared. Well, maybe at first it would, but soon after their brains would have forgotten it'd ever happened. That was all part and parcel of the magic of null and hidden zones. Now, if there'd been anyone around who was plastered or incredibly high, they may have seen the entire thing and not immediately forgotten it. It was one of the risks supers dealt with all the time when it came to portal travels and the various zones. The upshot, however, was those people typically either ignored the majority of what they thought they saw, were too far gone to comprehend what they saw, or remembered completely what they saw and upon telling someone about it ended up in the loony ward for a few months. That only needed to happen once before a person learned never to discuss the odd shit they saw when they were blitzed out of their minds.

Raina pulled into a parking spot and they got out.

Without waiting, she headed toward a lady who was wearing black shorts and a blue, collared shirt. The woman had very long, stark black hair that was perfectly straight. Her eyeglasses matched the color of her hair. They were thick and rounded, sitting atop a small nose that was slightly turned upward near the tip.

"Hey, Raina," the woman said.

"Hey, Kel. Have you seen Chief Fysh, by chance?"

"Not today, no. We were told she'd be coming in for a swim, but she never arrived." Kel gave Jin a quick once-over. "Hello."

"Hi."

"Oh, this is Chief Kannon," Raina said. "He's replacing Chief Fysh."

Kel got the look of someone who understood something. "Ah, so she's been kidnapped?"

"Yep."

Jin's face must have made it clear he thought the entire ordeal was super weird because Kel laughed. "It's an odd tradition with the cartel. Something that started in Laredo, I think?" She glanced at Raina, who nodded her agreement. "Yeah. Anyway, happens every time one of you guys is on the way out."

"One thing that would help," said Raina, "is to know if there've been any barrels of fish sent out someplace locally over the last few days."

That point made Jin more worried than he was before. "You think they cut up Chief Fysh and put her in a barrel?"

"What?" Raina then laughed. "Oh! No, fish as in f-i-s-h. Not F-y-s-h. I'm talking about actual fish here, not the chief."

"Ah. Whew." Then he frowned. "Why would knowing about a fish shipment help again?"

"Because Chief Fysh is a mermaid. She primarily eats fish."

That made sense, or at least he assumed it did. While Jin had tried his best to be well-read, he admittedly knew very little about mermaids. Come to think of it, he didn't know much about unicorns or wereroosters or leprechauns or cyclops or centaurs either. He knew far too much about succubi, though up until getting his PPD tattoo he'd not thought much about them in years.

Kel looked up from her tablet, which appeared quite different than Jin's datapad, and said, "Sure enough, three barrels left the supply room just two days ago." She held up a finger. "Before you ask, it doesn't say who took them or where they'd be going. However, if you look here..." she turned her tablet around... "you'll see they were packed into a white van by some people who were all masked."

"*Dogs*." Raina looked at Jin. "I'm talking about *The San Diego Dogs*, chief. That's the cartel."

"Right."

Turning the tablet back toward herself, Kel said, "Sorry, but that's all the information I have on this." She bounced her head this way and that for a moment, "If I was to hazard a guess, I'd say they took her to Hector's main house. He's the new head of the cartel, now that his dad's gone."

Raina jolted. "What?"

In response, Kel pulled down her glasses slightly, peering over them. "You didn't know that? Huh. You'd think of all the people in the area, the PPD would know when the head of *The Dogs* is no more."

Honestly, Jin was thinking the same thing. How would they not know this information? Maybe it was within the last few hours? Maybe they just hadn't been informed yet?

"How long ago did he die?" he asked.

Kel pursed her lips and said, "I want to say it's been about three months. Two, at least."

"No way," Raina said, her face contorted. "How'd they keep it from us for so long?"

"I was wondering the same thing."

"Me, too, Chief Kannon," Kel laughed. "Me, too." A device on the wall chimed. "Crap. Gotta run. The penguins have been ornery today and I'm on cleanup duty." She started heading up the path. "Nice meeting you, Chief Kannon. Good luck in your new role."

"Thanks."

As soon as they got back in the car, Raina turned toward him and said, "Doesn't seem right, does it?"

"I've been saying that since about seven o'clock this morning, Raina, so you'll have to be more specific."

"That they'd put Hector in charge of *The Dogs*," she

replied absently. "He's not exactly a tough guy. His dad was a monster, but Hector's more upbeat, almost positive."

"And you think that's a bad thing?"

She sniffed and then started the car. "Only if you're the new boss of a crime syndicate."

CHAPTER 17

Vestin

*J*anet Smith was a vision of perfection, at least her neck was. It was long and slim, the kind vampires found delectable. The rest of her was all business. Perfectly styled hair, a smart pantsuit that signaled she knew how to put herself together, and just the right amount of makeup to make you wonder if she was even wearing any while simultaneously recognizing no normal could look that flawless without at least *some* foundation.

Vestin caught the scent of something else in her blood, though. It was thin, almost imperceptible. She wasn't a pure normal. A vampire of lesser ability would never even have recognized it, but Vestin was *not* a vampire of lesser ability.

Pixie?

It would explain her impeccable skin, making him again rethink whether or not she was wearing makeup, though he wasn't sure why that mattered to him in the least. Maybe a subconscious process had kicked off because of her near-perfect looks that told him he was not dealing with a 100% normal here? Did that really matter? He supposed it all depended on precisely how much of Janet Smith's genetics were Pixie. Unfortunately, that was not something Vestin's advanced skills could determine.

"So you're the fucknut they call Dustin?" she asked, looking him over as if he was a peon.

The use of foul language and her inspection of him told a story of there either being far more pixie in her blood than he could sense or the fact that pixie DNA quickly dominated most everything else.

"My name is Vestin DeLanté," he corrected her, "though you may refer to me as Lord Vestin."

"Vestin it is." She walked around her desk and pushed a piece of paper across, setting a pen on top of it. "Sign that and we can get started. Don't, and you can take your little bat-ass back home."

He just stood staring at her, unsure of what to do. On the one hand, he wished to have a better marketing plan for *Shade* than…well, *Shade*; on the other hand, being treated thusly by an inferior was going to be taxing on his nerves. The document sitting on the edge of the desk would certainly contain a clause disallowing him to kill her. If he signed it, he would be beholden to its words. It was a DeLanté trait. Once they entered an agreement, they wouldn't break it unless there were simply no other options. They would push the limits until the *other* party broke the agreement, but that was different. Vestin's honor was paramount. Signing anything was going to put him into a relationship with a pixie-normal, and it would be a trying one.

"I know what you're thinking," Miss Smith said, "and you're right. You'll be giving up the ability to do anything to me. Why? Because I'm not a stupid shit, that's why. I've worked with the best of the best in the supernatural community, and I've learned over the years that you're all a bunch of backstabbing assholes." Did that mean she wasn't aware of her pixieness? "Fortunately, I'm a lot tougher than I look, which should be evident since I'm still around and a number of my past clients are nothing but worm food." She reached across and tapped on the paper. "Sign it, ya toothy dick, and we'll get started."

It took everything in him to walk over and pick up the paper. His first thought was to merely sign it and get started, but again he was not one who entered agreements lightly. They were binding to a vampire like Vestin. Therefore, he read it.

This agreement is between the Law Offices of Turner, Turner, and Smith, heretofore known as "The Offices", and Vestin DeLanté, heretofore known as "Fangboy."

The Offices will provide marketing services to Fangboy, incognito, sharing no internal details of his products with anyone, including law enforcement.

The Offices will use its best efforts to create an effective naming-convention for said products, claiming no ownership to the resultantly selected names, while being granted full ownership of all proposed names that are rejected by Fangboy.

Fangboy will not bite, kill, maim, or otherwise cause

physical or mental harm, either professionally or personally, to any employees or their families, immediate and extended, of The Offices during their time working together, and for an additional duration of no less than one thousand years after the close of business between the two parties, regardless of how the two parties disperse their relationship. Fangboy will also not hire, coerce, or otherwise engage anyone else to bring physical or mental harm under the terms listed above.

Further, Fangboy promises to recommend the services of The Offices over any other recommendation as it relates to marketing endeavors.

Fangboy will accept and understand that members of The Offices may, from time to time, refer to him bluntly and directly by the use of colorful names. The Offices accept and understand that this may cause challenging moments for Fangboy, but they're okay with that.

There were additional points running over the fifteen pages, which all but locked up Vestin's ability to do pretty much anything to Miss Smith, or anyone else associated to the firm.

If nothing else, he was impressed with their thoroughness. If they were even half as good with their actual marketing, it would be worth his signature.

But he had one remaining question.

"What guarantees do you offer?"

She crossed her arms. "None, of course. Duh."

He'd assumed that, but it had to be asked.

Part of him wanted to just set the pen down and jump across the desk, ripping Miss Smith's throat out in an act of defiance, but he sadly was forced to admit he needed their firm.

Or did he?

What difference did a name actually make in the grand scheme of things? Vestin was going to start his army regardless of what he ultimately decided to call his "product." Besides, in his estimation, *Shade* was a moniker he liked, no matter what his critics thought.

And therein lay the problem. His critics were the very people who were under the influence of *Shade* already. Well, at least Emiliano was under its geas. Prender wasn't, but that's only because he was already a dedicated follower of the mission.

The point was that if Vestin was to constantly hear rumblings about the name *Shade* it would be worth it to have something better. It may have been silly to most, but Vestin refused to go down in history as a leader who hadn't been flawless in his execution.

It mattered.

He signed it in his normal, flowery script and set the pen back down before bringing his eyes up to hers.

"What are the next steps?"

She took the paper, looked it over, counter-signed it, and then slid it into a glass cylinder before dropping it into a hole on her desk. There was a whooshing sound Vestin assumed meant the document had gone off on a journey to another department.

"The next steps are simple, you overgrown mosquito," said Janet, sitting in her leather chair, "I ask questions and you answer them."

"Right."

CHAPTER 18

Hector

"*L*isten, gang," Hector said as they walked into a hole-in-the-wall restaurant on the outskirts of town, "I'm really proud of how you handled the kidnapping and want to give you all a great meal. Before that, though, let's quickly talk about expanding our operation beyond drugs."

That statement caused quite a stir. *The Dogs* had always dealt in drugs. It was their specialty. Well, that and violence, but you typically just used violence when the drugs weren't moving properly, or if someone was stepping on your turf.

He allowed the mumbling to go back and forth for a few moments letting them vent their concerns to each other.

"Now, I know this sounds a bit different," he said finally, gaining their attention again, "but I assure you we won't be stopping the drugs." He turned and reached into his attache case, whispering, "At least not yet."

Some things were better left unsaid until a point was proven. Selling drugs needed no proof. It worked. The money poured in daily. What bothered Hector was the fact that drugs were rarely good for people, especially the kind his crew pushed.

Hector wanted the community to flourish. Mr. Becerra wanted the money to keep flowing. If Hector could manage a way to do both, his hope was that Mr. Becerra would not only love the idea but also adopt it for all the cartels in the area. Instead of being the "bad guys," they could actually do a lot of good, make a ton of cash, and there'd still be plenty of room for violence because when rival gangs came in trying to push drugs again, *The Dogs* would stop them, and those would be the kind of people Hector would want them to stop via violence. It would not only prove to his crew that he supported their ability to be themselves, it would show the community that *The Dogs* actually cared about keeping everyone safe and healthy.

Win-win-win.

The problem he faced was getting buy-in.

If he brought the concept to Mr. Becerra untested, he'd end up working the fields in the crazy heat. However, if he could get his crew to give it a shot—hoping none of them would snitch on him—it could be shown to be a grand money-maker. And if it failed, it failed. Hector hoped it wouldn't, but he was a realist. Okay, maybe an idealist with a realism streak, but he would accept it if things didn't go as expected.

Not trying was out of the question, though.

Taking a second to gather himself, he turned back to the table and started passing out laminated flyers.

The sheets looked great. They were multicolored, had many different products listed on them, and there were even set prices next to each so nobody would feel cheated. The prices were a bit high in his estimation, but the lady he'd worked with at *Turner, Turner, and Smith* said it was always smarter to charge more because it gave the buyer a sense of quality. She'd called him names like "Fido", "Buttsniffer", and "Tree Marker," but it'd been worth it due to the quality of work she'd provided. Besides, Hector's father had set up a running tab with that firm years ago so it wasn't like there was any other place Hector could go for this sort of work.

"Um, boss?" Sofia asked, raising her hand. "What's matcha?"

"It's a kind of tea that tastes like dirt," answered Cano before Hector could get a word out. Everyone looked at the henchman with baffled eyes. "What? I know things."

"Well done, Cano," Hector said, feeling just as perplexed as the others. "In addition to tasting like dirt, some people have attributed much value to the health benefits of matcha. It can have anti-inflammatory effects, there are antiviral properties, cardio protective benefits, and so on."

Sofia was still appearing confused. "That's swell, boss, but is the stuff addictive?"

"Not in the way Happy Product #7 is, no, but there is caffeine and people can certainly learn to rely on its effects. We all know how grumpy Alejandro gets before having his morning coffee."

Everyone nodded, looking somewhat grim at their run-ins with a non-caffeinated Alejandro.

For his part, Alejandro didn't seem to mind in the least. "I've warned everyone to stay away from me until I've had my third cup. It's on you if you come at me sooner than that."

They all acquiesced to that point, too. It wasn't wise to irritate Alejandro, even when he *was* filled with coffee. The man was large, seasoned in battle, and he loved confrontation. Hector was certain the coffee thing just gave Alejandro an excuse for whooping fellow cartel members who annoyed him too early in the morning.

The crew had gone back to studying their respective flyers.

"Just so I'm clear," Sofia piped up, not lifting her head from her reading, "we're going to try and push healthy stuff on people?"

"That's right." Hector started moving in an animated way to show how serious and excited he was about this idea. "I know it sounds crazy, but try to step back from what we've always done and think this through. Imagine a community where nobody is afraid of us. Instead, they can't wait to see us because we're protecting them from the ill effects of poor health and drugs."

"You mean instead of protecting them from what happens if they don't pay us to protect them?"

"Exactly, Alejandro." Hector was proud of the man. "Isn't that great?"

"No."

Fortunately, Hector didn't need everyone's full support. He just needed a majority or they'd run off and tell Mr. Becerra. If enough of them sided with Hector, he hoped the pressure of herd mentality would be sufficient to keep everyone quiet.

"Anyway," Hector pushed forward, "imagine people in the community actually *wanting* us to stop by. No more fear and crying, but rather the offer of a scone and tea."

Their frowning faces told Hector that wasn't the best carrot to dangle.

"…or maybe hot dogs and tequila?"

Their faces brightened considerably. It was often difficult to remember the audience for someone like Hector. He was Captain Motivation and his crew was built from people who were surly, tough, violent, and uneducated. It wasn't their fault, mostly. They'd not been given the options Hector had been. That's not to say everyone in the cartel fit those descriptors, or at least not all of those descriptors.

Alejandro aside, who only seemed to smile when he was inflicting pain, there were many people on the team who had demonstrated compassion. It was rare, sure, but Hector had seen it happen more than once.

And Cano was becoming more and more of a surprise with his knowledge of things he'd clearly tried to keep hidden from the rest of the squad. Hector understood why, too. Peers like these were brutal when they felt threatened. They teased and often kicked and punched if they believed you were acting as though you were better than them.

"The point, folks," Hector said, "is we're going to try

this plan. If it fails, it fails. No harm done. We learn and move on. But if it succeeds, we may well see ourselves ushering in a new era of income that not even drugs can touch." He paused to let that sink in. "Imagine how pleased Mr. Becerra will be if we're able to double or even triple our monthly earnings."

That regained their interest.

Sofia grimaced and said, "Spirulina?"

Again, Cano came to the rescue. "It's a biomass of cyanobacteria that's consumable by both humans and animals. There are three species: Arthrospira platensis, A. fusiformis, and A. maxima." His face was glowing as he spoke. "It's high in protein and provides a number of vitamins and minerals. In fact, it's been used for centuries in helping to deal with malnutrition and has been investigated as a potential dietary option for space flight and Mars missions!"

More confused looks followed.

"Who *are* you?" asked Sofia.

Cano's head merely fell forward, making him look defeated. Hector felt for the man, but it only further proved you had to know your audience.

"Good job, Cano," Hector said in support. "I believe I'm going to lean on you to manage training and leadership for our new product launches."

"Yeah?"

"Brown noser," Alejandro said.

"I think you mean 'green noser'," quipped Sofia.

Cano frowned at them both.

"Anyway," Hector said before the bickering could

begin, "do any of you have ideas that may improve this even more?"

"Cancel the idea right away and get back to selling drugs and busting kneecaps?" suggested Alejandro.

The others nodded their agreement. Everyone except for Cano, of course. He hesitantly raised his hand, obviously aware he'd be ridiculed again. "We could do one of those prepared food delivery things."

"Ah, you mean healthy meals?"

"Yeah. I mean, all we do anymore is eat fast food and so on. I'm not feeling as fit as I used to."

"You *could* stand to tighten up a bit," Sofia pointed out.

"Thanks for noticing."

"What? I see how your ass-cheeks move around like a—"

"Okay!" Hector bellowed before that conversation got too far out of hand. "Love the idea, Cano. Prepared food sounds great. We can probably even get the locals to help with it."

"Can force them to," noted Alejandro, a look of renewed interest creeping into his eyes. "It'd take a lot for me to eat something called 'spatualashitstain.'"

"It's spirulina, you dolt," Cano grumbled. Hector had heard him, but only because he was standing next to the man. If Alejandro had caught the insult, fists would be flying.

"Right." Hector cleared his throat. "Well, hopefully we won't have to force anyone, but I'll leave that to your discretion. Just remember that we're trying to build a community based on trust, not one that continues to harbor fear."

Alejandro groaned.

It was time to turn their attention to something they could all agree on.

"All this talk of food has me hungry." Hector clapped his hands. "I believe we have some nice chickens out in the backyard that are not only healthy, they make for some great tacos. What say we have a solid meal for once, instead of the fast food you all normally eat."

Everyone seemed pretty chuffed about that plan. At least that was something.

"Great. I'll talk to the chef. You guys keep sharing ideas." He clapped his hands and headed inside. "Nothing better than a fresh chicken!"

CHAPTER 19

Rudy

*R*udy had shifted into his wererooster form and was doing his best to keep his head in the game. It was always a struggle when there were a bunch of chickens around. There was something about the way the hens moved that acted as an aphrodisiac to him when his feathers were in bloom. The way they wiggled made him woozy. There wasn't much purpose for a wererooster to be in rooster form unless there were chickens around, though. The point was for him to blend in.

"You can do this, pal," Clive was saying through the connector. *"I know those feathers get your engine revving, but you have to do your best here to stay focused."*

"Thanks for the support, asshole. How's about we start with you not mentioning things like feathers?"

"Oh, right. Sorry."

It'd taken a fair bit of work for Miss Kane to alter the PPD tattoo and connector system in order to get everything working correctly for Rudy. Most of the other races didn't have much of a problem with it, with only a few tweaks here and there, but Miss Kane was quick to point out those supers were all of high intellect. Dealing with a "bird brain" made things somewhat trying.

Getting respect as a wererooster wasn't easy.

He pushed his way through the heap of chickens, trying not to rub up against any of them. All it would take was one touch and he'd turn into a fiend.

"Well, well, well," said an angry-looking rooster who stepped in front of Rudy, blocking his way. He was roughly Rudy's size and he had only one eye, making it clear he was tough. "What have we here? New guy coming in to strut his stuff, eh?"

Two other roosters, both younger, appeared out of nowhere.

"Fuck off, clucker," Rudy replied, knowing he had to show some gumption. "I'm on a mission here."

"Oh," said the apparent alpha as he glanced at the other two, "he's on a mission." They chuckled at their boss' use of sarcasm. "And what, pray tell, is your mission all about?"

"I'm not telling you that, you tiny-beaked one-eyed piece of baked turd-paste."

The underlings both looked shocked by what Rudy had said to their boss, but the big guy took it in stride. He was clearly not feeling the least bit threatened. That was a mistake.

"Why are you stopped?" asked Clive.

"Got three peckers here thinking I'm the new guy in town."

"You are."

"*Not what I mean, Mr. Ed. They think I'm here to fuck all the hens.*" He paused. "*I mean, I'd love to at least—*"

"Yeah, I get it. What do you want me to do?"

"*Got any tranqs?*"

"Yeah, Rudy, but they'll probably kill those roosters."

"*Your point?*"

Rudy wasn't one to care about things like that, at least not when it came to competition in the chicken yard. Even though he wasn't currently competing with these guys in the traditional sense roosters tended to compete, there was an underlying, animalistic feeling that he couldn't shake.

Regardless, they had to get out of his way, and fast.

"*Either you take them out with three silent shots or I take them out with my mad skills and draw the attention of* The Dogs. *Which do you prefer?*"

"*Shit.*"

It was an obvious choice, and it was clear that Clive had agreed when the two younger roosters fell over an instant after their feathers shot up in the air from the strike of Clive's miniature darts.

The boss rooster ducked, dropping down so his belly was flat on the ground.

"*I can't see the last one.*"

"*That's because he's hiding. Give me a sec.*"

Rudy stepped over to the older rooster and said, "Now that you know what you're dealing with, are you planning to stand in my way or are you going to shut the fuck up and take your new position in the yard? I can easily move all these lovely hens so my guy can get a clear shot, you know?"

"Who are you?"

"That doesn't matter. What *does* matter is whether or not you're going to be joining your pals in their slumber or if you're going to stay outta my way."

The guy sat there for a second thinking. It should've been an obvious choice, but Rudy sensed it wasn't.

"Guess I'll have to get up," the boss rooster said finally, though he was clearly struggling to get to his feet. "Better to be dead than to be relegated to watching while you run about having fun." He let out a ragged breath. "Don't get old, man."

"Wait," said Rudy. Then he added, *"Don't shoot until I tell you,"* to Clive. Focusing back on the boss rooster, he said, "Look, dude, I don't want you to lose your spot here. I'm just passing through on a mission, like I said. I'm not going to lie and say I wouldn't love to bed-down a few of these hens, but that's not why I'm here."

"Why *are* you here, then? I mean, what's your mission?"

"I've got to listen in on the humans and see what they're up to." He helped the boss rooster up. "Don't worry, I told my guy not to shoot you."

"Thanks."

"And your pals should be okay…maybe."

"Don't care if they are. Competition sucks."

"Right."

"The name's Luke, by the way."

Rudy nodded at him and decided to share his name. "Rudy."

"You're a wererooster, Rudy?"

That question threw Rudy for a loop. He'd never

known any regular rooster who knew about weres. To borrow Miss Kane's descriptor, most chickens *were* bird brains.

Unless…

"Are you a wererooster, Luke?"

"Nah, but I used to have a werehen succubus as a girlfriend."

Rudy's feathers shot up. "I never knew there was such a thing."

"Most amazing three months of my life, man," Luke said with a hint of melancholy. "She's the one who took my eye. Hurt like hell, but it was a great night."

"Oookay."

"Anyway, if you're a wererooster, that means your story about this being a mission holds up." Luke was back on his feet now and was moving to step aside. "I can tell you what they've been talking about already, if you want?"

Rudy paused. "Oh?"

"The main guy has been saying he's interested in branching out from selling drugs. Wants to sell health foods and supplements instead."

"Wow. Really?"

"That's what he said. I have a feeling we're all on the list of 'health foods,' though, based on what he said last."

"What did he say last?"

Luke looked around for a moment. "Oh, as to that it'd be easier if I showed you. Follow me."

They walked across and got close to the door at the back of the building. One loud squawk later and all the chickens cleared out, leaving only Luke and Rudy standing by the door.

"Why'd you do that?" Rudy asked as Luke took a few steps back.

The door swung open an instant later and a scrawny, older man reached out and picked up Rudy from the ground.

"Wererooster my ass," Luke called out. "A secret mission? You think I'm stupid, fucker?"

"Dude, not cool!"

"Up yours. Good luck on the chopping block, asshole!"

"*Shoot that asshole of a rooster, Clive!*"

"*Done. What happened?*"

"*They're going to eat me, that's what happened!*"

"*Fuck. What do I do?*"

Rudy was going into full panic mode here. In all his years as a wererooster he'd never once been put in such a situation. He'd always been clever enough to avoid it, but Luke had gotten the better of him. Son of a bitch, the guy was good.

It made him wonder if there actually had been such a thing as a werehensuccubus.

That would have to wait for another time. There were more pressing concerns to deal with at the moment.

"*I don't know, man,*" Rudy said, "*but I'm about to cause all sorts of a ruckus in here.*"

"*I'll go get the heavy artillery.*"

"*Yeah, you do that. Listen, if I don't see you again, well...you know.*"

"*You'll see me again, Rudy! Fight, man!*"

The chef walked into the back room where all the pans and knives were. That's when Rudy came face to face with Hector Leibowitz, the head of *The Dogs*.

"Yeah, that one looks fine," Hector said. "Might need one or two more, though. I've got a number of hungry soldiers out there. Just use that one as an appetizer."

An appetizer?!

"You got it, boss," said the chef as Hector walked out.

The moment the door shut behind him, the chef turned around to grab a large cutting knife. That's when Rudy focused all his energy into morphing back into his human form.

When the chef turned back around, Rudy reached out and snagged the chopping knife away and smashed it directly into the skull of the guy, causing him to fall backwards into one of the shelves that held a bunch of metallic bowls.

It was loud.

Rudy frantically searched the area for a way out, but there was nothing other than the chicken yard and that'd cause all sorts of havoc, so he focused again and turned back into a rooster.

Hector and a few of his goons burst into the kitchen a moment later.

"What the hell was that..." Hector paused looking down at the chef, who was no longer among the living.

"Magic chicken," said Alejandro, pointing a shaking finger at Rudy.

Hector gave him a look. "What?"

"Only a magic chicken can do something like that."

"*I'm coming in!*" Clive called out.

"*No, don't. They think I'm a magic chicken.*"

There was a solid five second pause. "*What's that again?*"

"I morphed, killed the chef, and morphed back. They came in and found the guy dead and now Alejandro is certain I'm a magic chicken. Obviously, that's bullshit. I'm a magic rooster."

"Huh." Clive paused again. *"I haven't seen Alejandro in a while. I thought he was dead."*

"Apparently not. Sofia and Cano are in here, too."

"Interesting. So, is Hector falling for it?"

Hector carefully studied Rudy for a few moments. "A magic chicken, eh? Probably shouldn't eat a magic chicken."

"Definitely shouldn't eat a magic chicken, boss," Alejandro agreed.

"I wouldn't," agreed Sofia.

Cano said nothing.

Rudy tail feathers shook whenever they referred to him as a "chicken." He was a goddamned ROOSTER!

"All right, well, I've kind of lost my appetite for chicken now." Hector pointed at Alejandro and then at Rudy. "Pick him up and bring him to my house. Let's get the witch to give him a once-over."

"Me?" Alejandro said, looking more than shocked. "Why me?"

"Because you're the one who is the most afraid of the chicken, that's why."

"But that makes no sense, boss!" Rudy had known Alejandro for a long time and he'd *never* seen the man like this before. "Have Sofia do it!"

"Fuck you, fuzz-farmer!"

Alejandro moved his finger toward Cano. "Him then!"

"Up yours, testes-tourist!"

"It's going to be you, Alejandro," said Hector, but he

was gentle about it. "I know you're the right person for the job. You fear the chicken, which means you'll be the only one who treats him carefully. I'll probably throw him out the window before getting back home. We both know that Sofia would just stab our feathered friend. And Cano —with what we've recently been learning about him— would probably figure out a way to eat it with some kind of marmalade sauce." He shook his head. "None of us make sense for this job. It'll be you, Alejandro. You'll take the magic chicken to the nice witch and we'll see what she says."

A nice witch? That was rare, and something told Rudy it was bullshit. But what could he do? If he morphed now, the jig would be up. Besides, if he went peacefully, maybe he could track exactly where Chief Fysh had been taken.

"I'll even let you ride with him in my limo," Hector said. "Think of it as a perk."

"Yeah, a perk." Alejandro didn't look all that convinced.

"*Okay, I'm going to go with them. Track my tattoo and let the others know what's going on.*"

"*You sure about this?*" asked Clive.

"*Nope, but I don't really see any other way to find the chief. Do you?*"

"*We already tried everything, so unless Raina and the new chief, or Lacy and Chimi have turned up something, this is probably our best bet.*"

"*Exactly. If nothing else, at least I'll get a limo ride out of it.*"

CHAPTER 20

Jin

$\mathcal{R}$aina suggested they go straight to Hector's and walk right in the front door. It seemed a bit reckless to someone who had spent his entire career hunting targets.

"They won't expect it," Raina said.

There was no arguing that point, but they would also be announcing themselves a bit prematurely. If Chief Fysh wasn't found at the new boss of *The Dogs'* main residence, it'd be clear the PPD was actively knocking on all the doors known to house members of the cartel. Based on the fact that it was all about tradition, this Hector guy would certainly be expecting the PPD to show up eventually anyway, but there were right and wrong ways to do things.

"Might be better if we're not overly brazen," he suggested, not wanting to force his position too heavily just yet. "If you're right, it might work out great; if you're not, it could jeopardize our ability to get Chief Fysh back because they'll have lookouts posted at the other safe houses."

Raina gave him a quick look. "Ah, right. They'll spot us and immediately move her out a back door and then off to another house. It'll be weeks of cat and mouse."

"That's my thinking."

"Makes sense, too. Good work, chief! You're a natural at this."

"Thanks."

He was a natural at stalking, but not for the reasons she was likely thinking. Then again, maybe her thoughts were dead on. His years of hunting targets made for certain ways of doing things, even if his brain was currently hiding the finer details.

Could be that the people who'd concocted his new mental script left in particular aspects, such as recon, sleuthing, and planning? It would make sense since he was a cop now. It'd be difficult to do a job like this without having at least a modicum of capabilities in the field. It was common sense. Without proper tracking and planning, an assassin would forever be trapped in heavy firefights instead of arriving to only deal with a few close guards. The same held true for a cop, at least he assumed that to be the case.

Jin *could* remember his last mission and that's precisely what'd happened there. Hinkers had his closest protectors around him. It did him no good at the end of the day, but it worked out well for Jin. Better to face those few than to face hordes of soldiers.

Another thing that helped a guy like Jin was reputation. That's what'd cleared many of Hinker's close guards out before the shooting began. He had no reputation in the San Diego PPD yet, though. Jin was nothing but the new guy. Part of him wanted to spread some information around town regarding how he'd left his role as a seasoned assassin in order to take this job. It was unlikely anyone up here would know about his past, and he would've been amazed if anyone had ever heard his name. People who lived topside tended not to care about the goings on in the Netherworld, especially the Badlands. But what if someone cared to look into him more deeply? It could backfire because they'd learn about his past targets, what methodologies he'd employed to take them out, and what frame of mind he was in now that he was a topsider.

All the supers would have to know he wasn't up here living with the same killer mentality he had before, though.

Right?

His own crew harbored concerns, so maybe not?

Somewhere in the recesses of his mind came the puffing out of his mental chest. It was as if his subconscious mind was saying, "Who cares if people know our tactics? We're amazing at what we do. Bring 'em on!"

The pain in his head was immediate.

It had to have been part of the integration.

There was a problem with the tough-guy bravado right now, anyway. Jin had limited recollection of his abilities. No, that wasn't exactly accurate. He believed he *knew* what he'd been capable of, even if just through basic knowledge of what an assassin could do, but he no longer had full access to it.

That didn't mean he was weak or timid or any of that.

He felt that to be true, anyway.

It was more a case of him needing to test himself in a real way, which would eventually happen. All he could hope for when it occurred was that he'd be capable of rising to the challenge, even if only to a degree that was necessary topside.

Since nobody up here would be allowed to get too powerful, it could be that his current skill level would prove more than sufficient.

"Guys?" Clive broke into Jin's thoughts, causing him to instantly grab for a gun. He quickly moved his hand away, recognizing it was going to take time to get used to this connector crap.

"What's up, Clive?" asked Raina.

She hadn't appeared to notice Jin's move. If she had, she was being kind enough not to say anything.

"Hector has Rudy."

That caused Jin to sit up. "Where is he?" He then shook his head and growled at himself, refocusing on *thinking* the words instead of *speaking* them. *"Where is he?"*

"I'm in a pretty posh limo," Rudy answered. *"It's just me and Hector. Well, and the driver, obviously. They think I'm a magic chicken."*

"What?"

"Long story. Anyway, they're taking me back to Hector's place to be interrogated by a witch."

Jin glanced over at Raina who kept her eyes on the road, but she was nodding her head.

"You know this witch?"

"I do, chief. Her name is Carina. She's going to be at Hector's main place."

"*Poor Rudy,*" Lacy chimed in. "*Yer prolly gonna end up in a soup bowl before this is after bein' over.*"

"*Shut up!*"

"*We're not going to let that happen, Rudy,*" Jin said in a tone that made clear they were *not* going to let that happen. It was strange for him to feel that way, indicating his integration was again at play. "*Are we, gang?*"

"*No, sir!*" It was a chorused response that sounded legitimate. Raina even sat up straighter when saying it.

Odd.

"*Good. Hang in there, Rudy. Play along with whatever they want until we get there and get you out. Got it?*"

"*Got it, chief. I have a feeling I'm okay, though, until they find out I'm a wererooster, anyway. Once that happens, they'll force me back into my human form and figure out I'm a cop. Then I'll be screwed.*" He made a strange sound. "*Shit. Okay, now I'm starting to worry again. Hurry up, you guys. I don't want them to find out I'm a cop!*"

"*We'll get there, Rudy!*" Clive yelled out.

Jin felt his heart racing. The last thing he wanted was to lose a member of his team, especially on day one. He'd already arrived too late to thwart the cartel's plan to abduct his predecessor. He wasn't about to lose two PPD members in one day.

Well, technically that'd already happened seeing that

Rudy was presently sitting in the back seat of a limo with one of *The Dogs*, but until they knew who they had at their side, it didn't count.

That's what Jin chose to believe, at least.

CHAPTER 21

Frannie

*C*hief Frannie Fysh should totally have seen the kidnapping coming, but she'd been so wrapped up in her job transition that she lost all sense of sensibility. There'd been a new chief arriving, she'd been promoted to Director, and she'd not had a decent swim in days. Plus, she'd had to think about her crew and how they'd react to everything.

And don't even get her started on the amount of paperwork that was involved.

So, yeah, thinking about the fact that *The Dogs* kidnapped outgoing chiefs hadn't exactly been in the forefront of her thoughts that morning.

Fortunately, soon after the guards had tucked her away in the dark room at Hector's command, the witch named Carina came in and let her back out. That, too, was at Hector's command. He'd always been a softy when it came to her.

Carina had taken Frannie down to the pool and cast a magic field to keep her inside.

As she basked in the indoor pool, she had to admit it was nice to get some much needed relaxation. If Frannie was going to have to endure being kidnapped, her current situation wasn't awful at all. If anything, it was kind of like hanging out at a day spa. There were no chains or blindfolds or anything like that. The room was magically sealed off, making it so she couldn't easily slip away, but even if she could, would she?

Frannie grimaced at herself.

Of course she would. There was duty involved here.

She snapped up another fish from the bucket near the edge of the pool and chomped down on it. They were relatively fresh, which was nice. Honestly, she'd spent so much time in her human form over the last few years that she'd kind of grown fond of the food normals ate. She still tended to order fish whenever she went out dining, but there were spices involved and the fish were cleaned and deboned. That wasn't a requirement for a mermaid, obviously. Still, she had grown accustomed to it, and she'd learned to love the deeper flavors.

Carina walked in to check on things, which she tended to do rather often. It was unnecessary. Frannie wasn't going anywhere. Her voice was magical, but it wasn't strong enough to bust through the kind of locks someone of Carina's caliber could manage.

Frannie knew the real reason Carina had returned to the pool room. The witch was lonely. And who could blame her? She never fit in with *The Dogs*. They were rough and ruthless. Carina wasn't into the darker forms of magic, even though she'd been forced to use them by the cartel. She was just as much a captive here as Frannie.

"Are you ever getting out of here, Carina?"

The witch took a seat on one of the lounge chairs and shrugged. "Where would I go?"

Where indeed?

She'd escaped the Netherworld because she'd been caught having relations with the husband of a jealous hellion. That was effectively a death sentence. Hellions were nasty creatures and they held a grudge until the grudge was obliterated. The guy she'd slept with had lost his marbles to his wife's knife, and then he'd lost his life choking on those marbles. As for Carina, she wisely rushed to the authorities in Netherworld Proper, finding herself aid there because she had helped them on numerous occasions. They worked on getting her into a relocation program, which landed her in San Diego.

Unfortunately, the leader of *The Dogs* at the time found out about her and threatened to contact the hellion unless she worked for him.

"Slaved" was probably a more accurate moniker.

It was a nasty arrangement, but part of Frannie couldn't help but think Carina deserved her fate. That probably came from the fact that Frannie despised cheaters. Mermaids generally avoided committed relationships, but when they landed in one loyalty was paramount. While Carina wasn't the one who had made the commitment, she knew better than to put herself in such a situation.

Actions came with consequences.

JOHN P. LOGSDON & JENN MITCHELL

The question now was how long was fair for punishment?

"Hector isn't as bad as his father," Frannie said, knowing that wasn't news to Carina. Regardless, it had to be said. There was a changing of the guard and Carina had an opportunity to take advantage of it. "Times change."

Carina nodded. "I know. Hector has always been good to me over the years."

"Probably because you've effectively acted like a mother to him, or at least an aunt."

"I've tried." She leaned forward a little. "Between you and me, I may have sent minuscule doses of positivity-based magic his way whenever we were together. I figured there would come a time when Emiliano was either forced into retirement or wound up dead, and that meant Hector would be the new alpha in town." She looked away. "Couldn't hurt to have someone leading *The Dogs* who had at least a hint of compassion."

So true.

"Your secret's safe with me, and frankly good on you for doing it." It explained why Hector had been so sweet early on in their relationship, though it didn't explain some of his more interesting choices when it came to playtime. "Just out of curiosity, did you—"

"No," Carina interrupted. "I would never tinker with someone's amorous desires. That's just who he is."

"Right." Frannie dipped under for a moment and came back up. "So why tell me this now? I've known you for many years, Carina."

"I…"

There was definitely fear in the eyes of the witch.

"Go on. You can tell me."

Carina hardened her resolve and looked directly at Frannie. "I don't want him to get hurt. As you said, he was like a son—or a nephew—to me. I've looked after him for so many years and I've invested a lot of myself into that boy. He's in a bad position, yes, but he has potential, you know?"

Frannie had to agree.

It was difficult for her to do so seeing as how they'd broken up and she still felt a bit of resentment over it. Hector had been a good boyfriend. Marriage material? Probably not, but that's only because of the mermaid thing. Committed relationship? For a time, maybe. They rarely fought and even when they did it'd always been Frannie fighting while Hector ended up being the one left to compromise.

Again, he'd been a good boyfriend.

The day Hector broke things off with her had come as a complete shock. He claimed they were just too different, but she knew it'd been Emiliano who had put his son up to it. That bastard was evil. Pure evil. He despised Frannie because she'd been the chief of the San Diego PPD, and even more so because she was a mermaid. Werewolves were persnickety regarding having relations outside of their own species. That's what confused Frannie most because Hector was the product of Emiliano's desire to play hide-the-sausage with a normal. And, yes, he was in human form when it happened. Not even Emiliano was *that* disturbed.

"He broke my heart," she said with a sigh.

"I know, but that only happened because—"

"Because his father was a complete jerk off. Yeah, I'm aware." She splashed her tail against the water. "It was stupid of me to get involved with a member of the cartel anyway. I'm a damn cop, for goodness sakes." She shook her head. "He was just so damned cute."

"And kind."

"Yeah, and kind."

"And positive."

"All right, all right. Cut it out before I get depressed again."

Carina smiled. "Sorry." The witch crossed her legs. "You know, now that Emiliano is dead, there's no reason you couldn't see if there's still a spark between you two."

Hmmm.

"Fair point. If you can see that, you should also see your situation has the potential to change."

"Yeah. I just don't know what I'd do." She swept her eyes around the room. "This has been my reality for a long time, Frannie. It's what I know now."

"Ah, bullshit. You're *not* the right witch for a job like this and you know it. You should just get out, find something that *does* suit you and make yourself a life you can be proud of." Frannie raised an eyebrow. "I *would* recommend you not sleep with any married men, though."

"Ouch."

"Sorry."

"No you're not."

"No," agreed Frannie, "I'm not."

They shared a laugh and slowly fell back into their own mental situations.

Frannie wasn't worried about Carina. She likely had the option of getting free from *The Dogs*, but it wasn't up to Frannie to force her to do it. The woman had to take those steps on her own.

It was kind of strange to see a witch in such a situation. They were usually quite in control of themselves. That only went to show if a person was beaten down enough they would eventually sink into their own personal cocoon and fade away, leaving behind who they once were.

But Frannie had seen the seemingly weakest people turn into absolute terrors when pushed too far.

That's why it was always the wise move to avoid poking the quiet ones. You never knew what kind of giant was sleeping behind the silence, and sometimes finding out was the last thing you did before one of the reapers arrived to take you to the Vortex.

"What's the new chief like?" asked Carina out of the blue.

"Don't know. I was thrown into the back of a van before I had a chance to meet him."

"Know anything about him at all?"

Frannie put her elbows up on the ledge of the pool and began a slow, rhythmic swishing of her tail fins. "Sure. He's from the Badlands. Just got his one thousandth kill for the Assassins' Guild. His name is Jin Kannon." As Frannie revealed more and more she noticed Carina's face growing whiter and whiter. "Do you know this guy or something?"

"Everyone who has ever lived in the Badlands knows Jin Kannon," Carina rasped. She then swallowed hard. "You sure he wasn't hired to come up here to find me?"

That was an odd question. "Pretty sure, yeah. I mean he got his one thousandth kill, so he was allowed to choose whatever he wanted. And even if that was all made up, why would anyone go through an integration process and join the police force if they just wanted to find a witch who left the Badlands ten years ago?"

"Money."

There *was* a lot of money in doing things like that, but Frannie still found it difficult to believe. The number of targets Kannon had taken out had to have provided him with a hefty chunk of change, unless he'd been notoriously bad at financial management. Of course, it could also be that he'd negotiated awful deals when finalizing contracts. There were a lot of people out there who undersold themselves all the time.

It still made no sense to Frannie, though his name *had* arrived pretty late into the game.

Could it be that the Guild had actually located Carina and subsequently sent up an assassin to take her out? That would be a pretty elaborate scheme, one that any assassin would have to make millions to go through, unless they were a masochist or something.

"I suppose you could be right," Frannie admitted, "but I'd seriously doubt it. For one, there are much easier ways to skirt the system. People do it all the time. It's one of the reasons there's a division of the PPD specifically set aside for Retrievers."

"That is true."

"Besides, hellions have a tendency of fighting their

own battles, or at least having someone from their own House do the dirty work for them. Hiring outside help is kind of rare."

Carina relaxed slightly. "You're right. Actually, I remember Linestra's words when she was caught in my slowing spell as I was running away. She said, 'I will tear you limb from limb with my bare hands, Helena!'" She looked up at Frannie. "That's my real name. Anyway, hellions tend to only make threats like that when they want nothing more than to enact the pain themselves."

"Yep. And they don't let go of grudges. Ever."

"No, they do not."

Frannie turned around and let the back of her head rest on the ledge. "Don't worry about the new chief. Even if he is looking for you, your name is Carina, not Helena, and the only two people who know that aren't going to tell a soul."

"Three people, actually," Carina said. "Emiliano was the third. Fortunately, he's dead now."

"Indeed."

CHAPTER 22

Rudy

$\mathcal{R}$udy still couldn't believe his luck. The whole "magic chicken" thing had started a long time ago when three ranking members in the Tucson branch all choked on the bones of a chicken at the exact same time. It'd turned out there'd been a local witch who had cast a spell on the chicken before it was taken back to the kitchen. Soon after there were incidents of where chickens would attack chefs, soldiers would have their eyes pecked out in the middle of the night, and various other poultry-related situations.

They finally found the witch and learned she'd been pissed because Mr. Becerra's predecessor, Mr. Lazon, had enjoyed a one-night stand with the woman's niece but never called her back. In standard cartel fashion, they attempted to assassinate her, but they soon learned that dealing with a genuine Dark Witch, advanced in her craft, was never a good idea. Mr. Lazon was found with his body bent and contorted to the point that his head was inserted into his ass. Next to him was a doll that had been bent into the same shape, along with a note that read, "Don't fuck with me, assholes, or I'll do even worse to you."

They wisely chose to *not* fuck with the witch; instead, they unceremoniously disposed of the body and put Mr. Becerra in charge of the cartel. He quickly sent a bouquet to the witch and another to her niece, apologizing for the acts of Mr. Lazon.

As tough as Mr. Becerra was, he wasn't stupid.

The story had become legendary, putting a deep level of fear into the members of the cartel.

Oh, they still worked with witches, but they were careful to choose ones who were against using dark magic and then made them use it anyway. The rationale was that they'd never use that kind of magic for their own purposes, although they could be forced to use it for the needs of the cartel. So far, it'd worked out just fine.

During the entire trip, Alejandro kept mumbling to himself. At first he was sitting as far away from Rudy as possible, but slowly he began to relax. Now and then he'd look down at Rudy, shake his head, look back out the window, and then mumble some more.

Finally, he pointed at Rudy. "You know what? I don't think you're a magic chicken!" It was said with such fervor, almost as if Alejandro was forcing himself to believe what he was saying. He was still shaking, though. "I think you're just a super lucky chicken who happened to be standing there when Chef Alvarez finally decided to do himself in." His finger was wagging now, but the shakes continued. "Everyone knows Alvarez was unhappy, and since Emiliano's death it'd only gotten worse. He probably overheard us talking about moving to these stupid healthy options instead of drugs, too. Then he got to thinking Hector wasn't gonna give him his weekly stash of pills and weed." Alejandro lowered his hand and glanced out the window again. "He was probably right, too. Oh, it'd take a while, but eventually Hector would get the poor bastard to start taking supplements instead. Likely we'll all be eating that crap soon enough."

Rudy was starting to worry. If this guy got it in his head that there wasn't a magic chicken riding in the limo with him, things could go south pretty quickly.

"Shit. If I have to drink that dirt crap every day, I'll probably join the damn chef." He glanced back at Rudy. "It *was* a pretty forceful way to kill himself, though, and that's what keeps bugging me. How could a guy take a chopping knife and slam it into his own forehead with such gusto?"

Alejandro was obviously still on the fence about things.

Rudy needed to push or he was going to end up on the wrong side of a fork.

The limo made a sudden turn, causing Rudy to slam against the side before jumping back to his feet. It hadn't exactly been an elegant look, and he found Alejandro was again squinting at him in curiosity.

In a flash, Alejandro sat straight up and turned his attention back outside. There was something about his look that Rudy knew all too well. He had the hots for someone out there and he'd not yet scored with her.

It was a guy thing.

"Ah, my sweet Ximena," Alejandro cooed, though the window was up, meaning she couldn't hear him. "One of these days, you will be in my bed."

Rudy fought the urge to gag at the thought.

"Perfection." Alejandro sighed, a longing look on his face. "She's a vision of perfection." He slowly grimaced and started in on a voice that made clear he was mockingly mimicking the woman. "'I only like men who have huge pythons in their pants. Do you have one of those, Alejandro? Hmmmmm?'" He grumbled to himself. "No, I don't have a huge python in my pants, but if I could just get five minutes with you, Ximena, you'd be pleased beyond belief." He sniffed and shrugged. "Or at least *I* would be."

The limo stopped and Alejandro stared at Rudy for a second. It was a stare that said he was going to have to look tough if he was going to step out in front of this Ximena chick. That meant he had to put aside his concerns about Rudy entirely.

"Bah! You're not a magic chicken. You're just a damn bird who got lucky." He reached out and snagged Rudy roughly. "We're going to put you on a spit tonight, you stupid shit."

The door opened before Rudy could morph, meaning he had to stay exactly as he was.

His mind was racing. He had to do something. Morphing at this point would get him killed pretty fast, and that would start an all out war between the cartel and the PPD. Not that Rudy would give a shit at that point, since he'd be dead and all, but he wasn't a fan of his legacy being scripted as the guy who'd kicked off a war.

Though there were worse legacies he could imagine. Like being the guy who was found with his dick in his hand and a belt around his neck in a posh hotel room or something.

Actually, maybe that would probably be better.

Regardless, there *had* to be something he could do!

"Hey, Ximena," Alejandro said in voice that was far more rugged than the one he'd been using in the car. "What's up?

She rolled her eyes at him. Rudy had to admit it was kinda hot. The dismissive attitude thing totally worked for a guy like Rudy, and apparently it wasn't lost on Alejandro either. On top of that, Rudy could definitely understand why the oaf was so taken by her. She was smokin' hot. Her curves alone were enough to make Rudy have to fight himself from morphing back and making a pass at her.

That's when it hit him.

He felt his eyes bulge as he looked up at the stammering Alejandro and then looked back at the beautiful Ximena, who had her arms crossed now.

Normally roosters made more of a "Buk buk buk bu-gawk!" type sound, but Rudy forced out a simple, "Big-cock!"

Ximena shot him a look, as did Alejandro.

He had to drive this home if he was going to live long enough for the rest of the PPD crew to arrive and get him out of this mess.

So, he went for it and pecked Alejandro on his side

and then looked straight at Ximena and repeated himself, mostly…

"Big big big big-cock!"

Alejandro looked back at Ximena who gave the man another once-over. It was almost a devouring appraisal.

"Big big big…Breallllllly big-cock!"

She smiled hungrily.

Alejandro's jaw dropped as he stared back down at Rudy with a look of amazement. "Wow, you really *are* a magic chicken."

CHAPTER 23

Clive

Clive parked away from Hector's house and waited for all the cartel cars to pull in before he made his move. It wasn't the first time Clive had been to the place, so he knew precisely where to get through their security.

He moved to the area around the back. There was a high, electric fence with razor wire at the top. It looked as impenetrable as Fort Knox, which meant guards tended not to worry about it all that much. Oh, they still did their walks through the spot, but it was only every thirty minutes or so, and since Clive was currently watching the back of a guard who was padding off into the distance, he knew he had time.

Summoning a bit of his Centaurian magic, Clive unzipped the back of his pants—yes, his pants had a zipper in the back—and his tail began to grow out, until it was at its full length. It was as hairy as a regular horse's tail, of course, but this one gave him some pretty nifty uses. With a bit of a push, he used it to catapult himself clear over the top of the fence. Then, once gravity had started pulling him back down to earth, he snaked it out and wrapped it around one of the limbs on a nearby tree. This allowed him a safe descent while keeping the noise low.

Still, he stuck to the shadows for a moment just to be sure nobody'd heard anything.

They hadn't.

Clive darted across the clearing and slipped through some thin trees that ran all the way to the top of the house. It made for the perfect cover for him to get up and look through the window near the top. It was also great because it allowed him to scale up the trees instead of fully elongating his tail.

If he was to go full-tail, he'd first have to neigh and that would definitely draw the attention of the guards, after knocking them all on their asses.

Clive's neighs were epic.

Using his tail, he pushed himself up along one of the trees and hung off it like a Christmas ornament, careful to keep the top from swaying. Things like that got noticed, after all. The last thing he needed was to get shot out of a tree. That wouldn't be a great first impression for the new chief.

The moment he looked in the window, two people walked in. The first was Emiliano's witch, Carina. She was a rare sight, even though Clive had surveyed the grounds many times over the years. He'd never had a chance to speak with her directly because there was nearly always someone with her, but the times he saw her made him think she wasn't happy being a part of the cartel. You'd think that would be true for most people. It wasn't. Many of the goons loved what they did. It gave them a level of power they'd probably never see anywhere else. Carina was always gloomy, though, like a person chained to the complex instead of being there of her own accord.

Behind her was a man Clive had never seen before. Either he was new to the cartel or he'd been hidden in one of the basement rooms over the years. The PPD was aware of the basement areas, and they knew there were people living down there, so it was a possibility. The guy wore a white coat, had a clipboard, a box of latex gloves, and a large bottle of lubricant.

Putting two and two together, Clive decided he was going to check out a different window…and fast.

But then a third person walked in and he was holding a large rooster out at arm's length.

It was Alejandro and Rudy.

"Hey, guys, I'm at Hector's place and I see Rudy," Clive called through the connector, purposefully omitting Rudy from the conversation so he wouldn't say anything that may break the rooster's concentration. *"There's a witch in there with him, and a doctor."*

"A doctor?" asked Raina.

"Yeah, I don't know the guy. Never seen him before. Has a bushy mustache and pork chop sideburns. Other than that, looks like a regular doctor to me."

"Is Rudy okay?" asked Chief Kannon.

"Looks okay, sir. I mean, I'm sure he's not thrilled with the situation, but he's...uh oh."

"What?"

"Um...well, sir, they've put him on the counter and the doctor is pulling on a latex glove. Now he's plopping his index finger into a big jar of lube. Now he's...oh man!"

"Buk buk buk...bu-fuck!"

Rudy's voice was clear as day, even through the window.

"What's happening, Clive?" demanded the new chief.

"The doctor's playing finger puppet with Rudy, sir!"

"Buk buk buk bu-Jesus-Christ!"

"He's after doin' what?" Lacy chimed in. *"Playin' finger puppet?"*

"Yeah," Clive replied. *"Checking Rudy's oil."*

"Huh?"

"Buk buk buk bu-for-the-love-of-all-that's-holy!"

Clive wanted to avert his gaze, just as both Alejandro and Carina were doing, but he couldn't. There were feathers flying everywhere and Rudy's eyes were bulging to the point where Clive thought certain they were going to pop out.

"What are you talking about?" That was Chimi. *"I don't understand how you change a chicken's oil. Wait! Do you mean they're cooking him?"*

"No!" Clive barked back. *"That'd probably be better! There's a doctor, like I said, and he's, well, giving Rudy the tunnel of truth tour. The internal high-five. Going for a treasure hunt in no man's land!"*

"Buk buk buk bu-how-long-is-this-gonna-fuckin'-

take?"

A moment later, Miss Kane entered the conversation. *"Clive, in his disturbingly childish way, is trying to tell you that the doctor—who is a veterinarian, by the way—is giving Rudy a rectal exam."*

"An exceedingly *thorough one,"* Clive added.

"Buk buk buk bu-does-this-mean-we're-dating-now?"

Finally, the doctor removed his finger and wrote something down on his chart. Clive was struggling to see it, but he couldn't until the guy spun the clipboard around to show it to the other people in the room.

"Okay, he pulled his finger free and wrote down something on his chart. I'm trying to read it..." He was squinting carefully, but it was difficult to see it from where he was. *"After...my...examination...I...conclude...this... is...a...rooster."*

"Buk buk buk bu...no-shit-I'm-a-rooster-you-fuckin'-prick!" They all jumped back and stared at Rudy for a moment. "Um...I mean...buk buk buk bu-gawk!"

Hector and Sofia walked into the room a moment later, taking everyone's attention off Rudy's outburst. That they'd not heard the other things he'd said during the entire "examination" was a testament to the fact they were too disturbed by the goings on to notice.

"Well?" asked Hector.

"Doc says it's a rooster," Alejandro said.

"It's obviously a rooster, Alejandro," Hector replied as if judging the man's intellect. "The question is whether or not it's a *magic* rooster."

The doctor wrote something down really quickly and spun it around.

"You felt something magical?" Hector asked, appearing confused.

"*Ew*," said Clive.

"Buk buk buk bu-perv."

They all looked at Rudy again. He was careful to keep himself facing the doctor.

"It may be best if I examine him instead," Carina stated. "If we are testing for magic, inserting fingers isn't going to help."

The doctor tapped on the words he'd just shown everyone on the clipboard.

Carina gave him a sour look. "You have issues, Dr. Sanchez." He wiggled his eyebrows. "Anyway, I need a few minutes alone with the bird in order to determine if there is any magic involved here."

She shuffled them out the door and walked toward the window. Clive moved to the side, but Carina opened it and said, "You may as well join us. I'm actually surprised nobody saw you other than me." She paused a moment. "Then again, after what we all just witnessed, maybe that's not surprising."

Clive sighed and climbed in, after making his tail disappear.

"One second," Carina said, bringing magic to her hands. She then put her hands on Rudy and he instantly relaxed. "There, that should do it."

"Buk buk buk bu-whew."

"You can go ahead and morph back into your normal self, Captain Valdez." Clive's eyes shot open wide at her words. So did Rudy's. "Yes, I know who you are. Honestly, I *didn't* know until I saw your partner's face after the doctor took his finger out of your…well…you know."

"Buk buk buk bu-boy-do-I."

A few seconds later, Rudy was back to his normal self, and he didn't look happy. Not that anyone could blame him. That doctor was messed up.

"I'm going to kill that guy," Rudy said.

Carina put a hand on his shoulder to calm him down. "He thought you were a chicken…a rooster. I did, too. If he had known you were a wererooster, he never would have done that. And if I had figured it out sooner, I wouldn't have let him."

"Somehow that doesn't make me feel any better," Rudy replied. "I mean, does he do this to all the animals?"

"Among other things, sure. He's a vet."

"I know of no branch in the military where—"

"No, a veterinarian."

"Oh, right. Still, there aren't—"

"It's normal procedure for doctors of his kind to check various aspects of the animal, Captain Valdez." She was keeping calm, even though Rudy was obviously quite fired up. "Again, if he had known what you truly were, he probably wouldn't have done that."

"Probably?"

"Anyway, you obviously *are* a 'magic chicken,' even if they were mistaken as to what kind. It's fortunate for you that Ty wasn't able to discern what you truly are."

"Ty?" asked Clive.

"Sorry, yes. Dr. Ty Sanchez."

Rudy put his hands on his hips. "Are you shitting me? Dr. Ty Sanchez? DRTY SANCHEZ!"

Carina stepped back, clearly shocked by Rudy's proclamation. "Wow. I never considered that. Makes you think, doesn't it?"

Clive had to hold Rudy back from running out the door to hunt down the good doctor. That wouldn't do anyone any good, except maybe Rudy, even if only briefly.

"I *am* sorry for what happened," Carina said. "Ty is actually a pretty decent veterinarian. He's thorough."

"You can say that again."

"Sadly, he's incapable of talking, but he claims the animals speak to him."

"Yeah, and I'll bet the only word he ever hears is, 'Nooooo!'" Rudy harrumphed. "Fucker."

"*Is everything okay?*" Chief Kannon called through. "*You've been quiet for too long. We've just arrived.*"

"*Carnia—that's the witch—knows about Rudy, but she's not said anything to Hector or the others. They're not in the room anymore. I am, but they're out waiting for Carina to give her report.*"

"*Is he okay?*"

"*He's not thrilled but Carina...um...soothed things.*" Clive cleared his throat. "*I would say it'd be a good idea to drive up. That will get Hector's attention and Rudy and I can sneak through to find Chief Fysh.*"

"*Got it. Driving in now.*"

"The new chief is here with everyone else. I've told them to drive in." Clive then nodded at Rudy. "You should probably change back into a rooster and I'll hide behind that chest over there."

"Okay, but if that doctor comes back in here with his finger at the ready, I'm *going* to kill him."

"He won't," Carina assured him. "Once I've told everyone what they need to hear, they'll leave and you can go on about your business."

"We need to find Chief Fysh," Clive said. "That's why we're here."

"I assumed as much. She's in the main pool area." Carina walked to the door and looked back briefly. "I'll make this quick and then we'll get your chief."

CHAPTER 24

Vestin

*V*estin opened his email and found something from Janet Smith. He was somewhat excited to see what they'd come up with, though he was a bit worried because both Prender and Emiliano were standing in his office awaiting orders. On the one hand, he could easily have shooed them away; on the other hand, having their opinions might not be such a terrible thing, especially if what the agency had come up with was abysmal. It was always nice to have someone to blame, and Emiliano *had* been the one to recommend Miss Smith and her company.

Somewhat pensively, he clicked to open the email and did a quick scan.

"Something wrong, My Lord?" asked Prender

"I've just received the first-pass of names for the-product-previously-known-as-Shade," he replied a bit tersely. "I must say I'm not impressed."

"Oh?"

"Her first suggestion is to call it BTD."

Prender scratched the back of his head. "Beeteedee? It would be better maybe as Beetahdah!"

Vestin looked over the top of the laptop screen at his second-in-command, worried he may have chosen poorly.

"The *initials* are B-T-D, Prender."

"Ah! Yes, I see." Then Prender tilted his head to the side. "*Big Toothed Dudes?*"

"What?"

"I was thinking *Barf Turd Diabetes*," offered Emiliano, "but I'll fully admit that—as a zombie—I sometimes have very odd thoughts now."

Honestly, if these two were his primary commanders, Vestin was in trouble. They were clearly good at being the muscle. Well, Emiliano carried that reputation anyway. Vestin wasn't so sure about Prender. His resume showed he'd been a leader in several campaigns over his years but that didn't mean he was *good* at it, and thinking BTD would mean *Big Toothed Dudes* was just asinine.

It was too late to change direction at this point, though. Training new commanders was never easy. He hated to do it, in fact. If nothing else, Prender had become rather efficient at picking up Vestin's dry cleaning and making him a solid blood-coffee.

"It means *Bite Transmitted Disease*, gentlemen."

"Oh."

They both grimaced and gave each other looks of distaste.

"I know what you're both thinking, and I would tend to agree. Not only does it sound dirty, it's not going to tempt many people into being interested in learning more."

He scrolled further down and saw other names like *Fang Fetish Fanaticification* and *Gripping Garlic Gagger*. Nothing looked even remotely interesting, until he reached the very last one on the list. It still wasn't great, but it was definitely better than the rest, making him think Miss Smith had saved the best for last.

It was a common tactic.

As he read it over and over, it began to grow on him. That probably had to do with the use of the word *Shade*, which was his original title for the venom.

"What do you two think of *Shaded Past #13*?"

Their responses weren't immediate. They looked to be weighing the name carefully, allowing themselves minor nods and eyebrow lifts. The two men even glanced back and forth at each other more than once, possibly hoping to catch a feeling that may sway them in one direction or another.

"I kinda like it...My Lord," Emiliano said first. "I didn't know there'd been thirteen iterations of the stuff."

"There haven't been," Vestin replied. He then looked at Prender. "And you?"

"I believe I was the first iteration of—"

"What do you think of the *name*, Prender?"

"Ah, yes. Right. Sorry." He was holding his chin in his hand. "I rather like it, My Lord. It has a bit of pizazz to it, you know?"

He didn't. If anything, Vestin thought it sounded like

some kind of special product that took away all your worries from the past.

Hmmm.

He looked at the image under the name, finding it rather interesting.

Shaded Past #13

Vestin showed it to the others and they both smiled. On Prender that looked fine, but on Emiliano, who was missing a good portion of his jaw and teeth, it was super creepy.

"Love it," Emiliano said, leaving off the honorific as he held up the flyer and read it a few times over.

"I agree," said Prender after Emiliano handed him the card. "These are truly wonderful, My Lord. If we set up a place where people can pick up their supplies, we could have an army built in no time."

"You think?" Vestin asked. He didn't feel so sure about it, but he had to admit he wasn't the best at this side of the game. Vestin was a doer, not a marketer. "Fine. Prender, you'll be in charge of finding us a location that can't be traced back to me. It will need to be large enough to house at least one hundred people and I'll need a room where I can administer the venom directly." He pointed sternly at his second-in-command. "Nothing cheap, Prender. I don't enjoy working in slovenly surroundings."

Prender bowed his head. "As you say, My Lord."

"As for you, Emiliano, go and get as many of your old guards as you can and bring them back. We will need more ruthless killers for this to work."

"No problem...um...My Lord."

CHAPTER 25

Jin

J in wasn't sure what to expect when they pulled into the complex. It looked like a mansion that was loaded with guards, all carrying weapons. Way in the back of his brain he felt bad for each of those guards, knowing that he could drop all of them without a second thought.

A pain stabbed him right above the eye, causing him to wince.

"You okay, chief?" asked Raina.

"Yeah, just…" He rubbed his forehead for a second as the pain subsided. "Apparently the integration is providing me with some side-effects."

"Ah, right. That happens." She waved at a few of the guards while pulling up to the main parking area. "I should say I've *heard* it happens. I've never had any issues, personally, except that one time they tried to reintegrate me during the full moon." Raina put the car in park and let out a sigh. "Anyway, I try not to think about things like that." She looked in the rear view mirror. "Lacy and Chimi are here, too."

She got out of the car leaving Jin to wonder what was going to happen whenever they actually got to a full moon. He had some basic information, but there was nothing like firsthand experience to really understand how good or bad something could be. Having known Raina only a short period of time, he couldn't give a complete psychological profile, but his initial impressions, coupled with how everyone treated her, made it clear that she was upbeat, positive, and downright likable.

Could there really be some kind of horrible event during the full moon that might jeopardize his view of her? He couldn't imagine it, if so.

After crawling out of the vehicle, Jin found himself looking at the wrong side of gun barrels.

"It's okay, chief," Raina called over to him. "You just want to leave your guns in the car and make sure you don't have any other weapons on you."

He was about to comply when another voice sounded.

"The new chief may keep his weapons." Turning toward the voice, Jin saw a younger man who was surrounded by guards. He was coming out the front door of the extravagant house. "It's a pleasure to meet you, Chief Kannon. I'm Hector Leibowitz."

Jin said, "*Leibowitz?*" through the connector.

"*It's complicated,*" came the unified response from his team.

"Nice to meet you as well, Mr. Leibowitz."

"My friends call me Hector."

Jin inclined his head.

He wasn't so sure he wanted to be too friendly with the cartel, but there was always a fine line that needed to be walked, at least according to the cop shows he'd watched now and then in the Badlands. Down there, episodes from shows like *Blood Murder Neck Crank* usually started out with lots of blood, murder, and…well…neck cranks.

Anyway, the point was he was glad there hadn't been any bloodshed so far, and he hoped to keep it that way.

Damn, that integration stuff was strong.

"I'm assuming you know why we're here?" Jin asked.

"To rescue Chief Fysh, no doubt," replied Hector as if it was nothing. "She's fine, I assure you."

"Found the chief…erm Director, chief," Clive interrupted Jin's thoughts a moment later. *"She's chilling out in a super nice pool here, eating fish. The witch helped us find her, but you might not want to tell anyone that."*

"I'm not my father, Chief Kannon." Jin was going to offer up his first name as an option, too, but decided to forego it. Hector's eye twitched slightly. "He was one who put previous chiefs in chains and stuck them in a dungeon until they were found—which often took weeks." Jin glanced at Raina, who affirmed the story with a nod. "I, on the other hand, am merely keeping with the traditions set forth by those who precede me. *How* I go about enacting the tradition is entirely my call."

"The nuances anyway," said the guard next to him.

"Yes, Sofia. Thank you for the clarification."

There was obviously a bit of contention in that relationship. No doubt she was Hector's father's main guard before and she wasn't thrilled with the new direction Hector was taking. While Jin didn't know her personally, he knew her type. They generally enjoyed their roles dominating others.

Jin moved his gaze to the taller guard on the left. He was rugged, scarred, and his eyes told the tale of a man who thoroughly loved crushing people. The guy's knuckles were calloused, as well. It was highly probable that more than one set of teeth had been lost in the building of those callouses.

If the shit ended up going down at some point, those two guards were going to be the biggest challenge, at least from the ones Jin had seen thus far. A few others stood out, such as the one standing directly behind Sofia, but none of them looked nearly as tough. Jin had been fooled before, though. Besides, if even one episode of *Blood Murder Neck Crank* was remotely accurate in the grand scheme of things, it was the ones who looked the most expendable who ended up owning your shit. That tended to happen because they were easily overlooked. They were non-threatening, comparatively. So as you went after the tougher types, you soon found multiple knives hanging out of your back.

The door opened again and out stepped Rudy, Clive, and an incredibly beautiful woman who had long wet hair.

It had to be Chief Fysh...or was it Director Fysh now?

"Ah, there she is," Hector said, spinning around. He jolted slightly. "How did you two get in my house?"

Rudy stepped right up to Hector and started poking

him in the chest. The guards looked confused about what to do.

"What the fuck, dude?" Rudy said. "Dr. Ty Sanchez?"

"Um…yes?"

"DRTY SANCHEZ!?!?"

Hector stepped back and said, "Huh. I've never thought of it that way."

"Yeah, well…he's…uh…"

"*Careful, Rudy*," Raina said through the connector, "*unless you want them to know your secret.*"

Rudy gritted his teeth. "He's not nice to animals!"

"But he's a veterinarian," Hector replied. "I don't understand what…" That's when Hector stopped and watched as a lone feather fell from Rudy's jacket. Slowly, he brought his eyes back up. "You're a wererooster?"

"Shit."

"*So much for gettin' after usin' that spyin' tactic again, ya feathery fart.*"

"*Thanks, Lacy,*" Rudy growled in response. "*I wasn't sure. Glad you were here to point it out. What would we possibly do without you?*"

"*Nay a problem. Doin' me bit, is all.*"

Sofia and the larger guard were both laughing, or doing their best to hide the fact that they were laughing.

"Get you an ice cube, pal?"

"Fuck you, Alejandro," Rudy snapped. He then turned to Sofia and added, "That goes double for you."

Alejandro laughed a little harder and then blurted, "Buk buk buk bu-my-bad!"

Clive had to hold back Rudy, which was probably a good thing since Alejandro would undoubtedly have ripped the dude apart. As for Hector, he showed actual compassion for Rudy's situation. He even tsk-tsk'd his guards.

Then, Hector put his hand out toward Chief Fysh. The way she took his proffered hand told Jin there'd been more to their relationship than PPD chief vs. cartel boss.

He decided to keep that to himself.

Hector waved at his guards, causing them to lower their weapons and stand at ease. The level of control he held over them was impressive, which made Jin wonder if there was more of a ruthless streak in the guy than the PPD knew about. Some people were great at playing a role of benevolence in public, but when they got behind closed doors they were downright dastardly.

If that were the case, though, would Frannie Fysh be so quick to take Hector's hand?

Doubtful.

Her record was clear.

She was tough and didn't take shit from anyone. There was even mention in the folder Jin had read where Chief Fysh had singlehandedly wiped out eight armed bandits who'd tried to storm Sea World on her day off. They were pixies, too. Anyone who has ever underestimated a pixie wouldn't say a word about it, because they'd be incapable of doing so, unless, of course, you were with them on the other side of the Vortex.

"Here you go, Chief Kannon," Hector said, letting go of Chief Fysh's hand. "No harm, no foul."

"Maybe *some* harm to *some* fowl," Alejandro quipped, causing him and Sofia to bust out laughing again.

Clive dragged Rudy away. "Let's go. The big idiot's not worth it."

"Hey, Sofia," Alejandro said, "if you were to eat one of Dr. Sanchez's fingers, what would you say?"

"Tastes like chicken?" she replied. They laughed again, and a number of the other guards did as well. Then Sofia quickly added, "Gives an entirely new meaning to the term 'Chicken Fingers,' too!"

That sent everyone into a frenzy, aside from Hector and the PPD crew, of course. Clive was doing his best to hold Rudy back. Jin assumed the strength of a centaur bested that of a rooster, even in human form.

Hector spun and pointed at his two guards. "Enough out of you both!" He then gave a quick bow toward Rudy. "I obviously did not see what happened, but I can imagine and I'm terribly sorry." Hector then put up his hands and said, "You *could* have morphed before it happened, though."

"And you wouldn't have had me killed in a heartbeat?" Rudy challenged.

"I'll say it again…I'm not my father."

"Out of curiosity," asked Jin, "why do you have a veterinarian on your campus, anyway?"

"We're werewolves, Chief Kannon. We need looking after just like everyone else."

At that admission, Rudy yelled out. "No fucking way! You dick-inspectors have been getting third-knuckled for years by that guy and you're giving *me* shit about it?"

The laughing stopped.

"Oh, yeah," Rudy said, relaxing enough that Clive let

him go. "Let me guess, you're all getting your anal glands expressed because they keep getting impacted?" He pointed up at Alejandro. "I'm sure yours gets impacted the most."

"Sounds wrong," mumbled Clive.

Rudy ignored him. "You probably get back in line three or four times on cheek-pokin' day, Alejandro. Don't ya?"

Alejandro growled as his lip turned into the shape of a snarl.

"That's enough, Captain Valdez," Jin found himself saying, though he wasn't sure why. The truth was Rudy had the right to mock back some, after all he'd been through. It wouldn't help the relations between the cartel and the PPD, though, and Jin had the feeling he needed that in order to keep the peace in San Diego. "You've had your say."

"One more, chief and I'll let it go." Rudy didn't hesitate before adding, "Bet ya got neutered, too, didn't ya big boy?" That's when Ximena walked into the yard. "Oh, hey Ximena. Remember me? I'm the rooster that Alesmallbelow was holding when he got out of the limo." She looked confused. Alejandro looked terrified. "I just happened to have seen Alejandro naked and he's got the tiniest little wink-wink I've ever seen. It's adorbs. He should name it Mr. Widdle Pokey or something."

Ximena covered her mouth, obviously holding back a laugh.

Alejandro began to rush Rudy when Hector barked out, "ALEJANDRO, SIT!"

An instant later, Alejandro was sitting on the side of

the small hill, looking utterly baffled at how that'd happened. It appeared Hector had some definite power over his guards. The most interesting part was how Hector, too, appeared to be shocked by the effects of his voice.

He quickly gathered himself, however, and turned back toward Jin. "Now, I believe the next step in this is for you to take me, Sofia, Cano, and Alejandro downtown, yes?"

Jin looked at the previous chief and she shrugged. "You're going to be the new chief soon, Kannon, so I'll let you make the call."

"Right." He took off his hat and ran his fingers around the brim. "Well, it doesn't appear there was any real harm done."

"I beg to differ," noted Rudy.

"Sorry, no *intentional* harm done." He continued quickly. "And it seems as though Director Fysh—it is Director now, right?"

"Not until you've been sworn in."

"Miss Kane did the honors earlier," Raina pointed out.

Frannie said, "Huh. Okay, then. Yep, if you're the new chief, then I'm officially a Director. Paperwork only said you had to be sworn in for me to assume the new title. Since that's done, well, welcome aboard Chief Kannon."

Jin glanced around, feeling it was an odd place for this to happen. "Uh…thanks. Congrats on your promotion." He cleared his throat. "Anyway, since *Director* Fysh is fine, I think we'll just call it a day and hope that this will help set the tone for our relationship going forward."

With that, he reached out his hand to Hector.

The new head of the cartel took it and smiled.

Friendship between the cops and the cartel? What could possibly go wrong?

CHAPTER 26

Emiliano

$\mathcal{H}$e stood at the edge of the property with a number of zombies under his command. They were on the hilltop near the side of the house, which gave them a perfect view down into the goings on between his son and the San Diego Paranormal Police Department.

"Disgusting," he hissed.

"What is, Leader?" asked Shiela, the zombie who had stayed close to him the entire trip over.

Was she afraid, aroused, or just jockeying for position in the new army? Emiliano couldn't say, but in his current physical form he somewhat doubted aroused would be a possibility. Then again, they were both zombies now, so maybe?

Ugh.

She'd been one of the newer guards for *The Dogs*, if he recalled correctly. The last few months were a bit of a blur. There'd been a lot of pain as his body fought to reanimate itself, and he'd been awake through all of it, including the burial and the pathetic way his son, Hector, had cried.

What kind of cartel kingpin cries at a funeral? Deaths offered opportunities, since it meant positions of power became open.

That was no crying matter.

"Disgusting," he repeated, not bothering to answer Shiela's original question.

He turned, pushing her away. That garnered everyone's attention. Even if they were already dead, they knew power when they saw it, and Emiliano radiated the stuff.

"We're going to go down there to rip those damn cops to pieces. Do you hear me?"

"Yes, Leader," they replied as one, though it was raspy and nearly silent.

"Kill the cops, but do not kill any of the cartel members. Just disarm them, knock them senseless, and we'll drag back as many as we can to our Lord."

"Yes, Leader."

Emiliano despised referring to the vampire as "Lord," but he couldn't help himself. Whatever power the dirty-fanged fool held was more than even he could withstand. It irked him to no end. Sadly, he could do nothing about it.

"I will take care of Hector," he added. "Anyone who touches him will be mincemeat."

After looking each of them directly in the eyes to affirm they knew he wasn't messing around, Emiliano turned and jumped over the high fence, clearing it with no problem. His new, zombified body had provided him with an entirely new level of physical strength.

They all landed in near silence a few moments later.

While Emiliano could hear every word, every snap of a twig, every bending blade of grass...not a single cop or guard even looked their way when they hit the ground.

Impressive.

Waving his hand forward, he felt his blood, or whatever was running through his veins, start to boil.

It felt amazing.

"Let's kill!"

CHAPTER 27

Jin

*R*ight as they were getting back into their cars, the shit hit the fan. Out of nowhere, a mass of zombie-looking creatures had rushed in and started punching Hector's guards.

Jin had never seen such beasts before. He'd seen zombies, but not this kind. They were easily a full head taller than anyone on the campus, and that included Alejandro. They had patches of flesh hanging off their bodies, gaping holes in their chests, abdomens, and faces, and they had huge claws that Jin assumed were razor sharp.

"What the intercourse are those?" cried Chimi, clearly shocked but not enough to use the word "fuck."

Lacey replied with, "Somethin' I'll be after flyin' way up here to avoid!"

Raina reached into the window of her car and did something to cause the trunk to pop open. She darted back and pulled out a weapon that caused Jin to reevaluate his deputy.

"Is that an M134 Minigun?" he asked.

"Wow, chief," she said, looking as surprised at him as he was with her. "You know your guns, don't you?" She then blinked a few times. "Actually, I suppose that makes sense seeing that you were an assassin and all."

True, but it wasn't the reason he knew that particular weapon. It was more a case of *Predator* being one of his favorite all-time topside films. Jin had just never seen one of the little beasts in person.

"Look out!" Raina yelled, causing Jin to hit the dirt immediately.

It seemed some things had stuck with him, even after integration.

An instant later, there was the brrrrrrrt sound of that M134, followed by a fine mist of zombie juice coating Jin's coat, along with a number of chunks. It was gross, but it proved the effectiveness of that weapon.

"Got any more of those?" he asked, jumping back to his feet, wiping himself off as best he could, and then grabbing his own guns out.

"Just the one." She patted its side. "I've had Bernadette since my cadet days."

Jin couldn't help but wonder how the PPD would allow a cadet to have such a weapon, but he sure was glad they had.

By now, the zombies had dropped most of the guards and had turned their attention toward the PPD, Hector, Sofia, Cano, and Alejandro. They were the only ones still standing. After seeing what Raina's gun could do, however, they dared not charge in.

The largest of the zombies stepped up and grabbed two of the others, pulling them to stand directly in front of him. It was like he was using them as shields.

Smart. Disturbing, and probably pointless against "Bernadette," but still smart.

"My boy," the zombie said in a gurgling voice while looking at Hector, "you disappoint me yet again."

"Emiliano?" said Sofia, Cano, Alejandro, and all the PPD cops at the same time.

Hector's face was ashen as he stumbled back, using Raina's car as a prop to hold himself up. "Father?"

"I'd prefer you didn't use that term with me any longer," said Emiliano. "Making friends with the cops? Really?" He shook his head like any disappointed father would do. "Disgusting."

"But…how?"

"That's what *I'd* like to know!" Emiliano's cheek flesh was waving in the wind. "In all my years running *The Dogs*, I would never have even *considered* making friends with the cops, and *you're* asking *me* how to do it?"

"Huh?" Hector closed his eyes for a moment. "No, I'm asking how you're still alive?"

"Oh! Right. Well, that happened because—"

One of the two zombies Emiliano had been using as a shield interrupted him, saying, "Leader, you're not supposed to say anything about that, remember?"

He snarled at her for a moment and then relaxed. "True, but don't interrupt me while I'm speaking. Pet peeve of mine that will surely cost you your life...in a manner of speaking."

"Sorry, Leader."

The guy next to her said, "How are we supposed to stop you from saying something stupid if we're not allowed to interrupt you?"

Three seconds later, the guy was lying on the ground about twenty feet away with his head facing the completely wrong direction. Emiliano reached out and grabbed another zombie to take his place.

"You got any smart ass questions?" he asked the new guy.

"No, Leader. I only have a compliment. You're the best Leader a follower could have. I've seen many a leader in my day, but none as solid, strong, and...uh...smart as you, Leader."

"Well said," Emiliano replied, patting the man on his head, which caused only a hint of crushing. He looked back up, focusing on Hector but still talking to the guard whose skull he'd just dented. "It's a shame *you* weren't my son."

"It would've been a dream come true, Leader."

"Silence!"

While this display was going on, Jin was well aware of how the zombies were moving to surround everyone. They were taking steps to make sure Bernadette couldn't hit them all.

That left quite a few to serve as fodder, but Jin had the feeling Emiliano was okay with that.

"*You guys are catching on to the fact that they're planning to take Raina's gun out of the equation, right?"* he said through the connector.

"I'll still take three or four of them out before that happens, including Emiliano."

That would leave only a few, assuming she could actually knock out that many in time. If not, they were going to be in a world of hurt.

Jin attempted to access his magic. It was still there, though it didn't fit the memory of what he'd felt back at Hinkers' place. This wasn't even twenty percent of the power he'd accessed there. Still, he had to see if he could move as quickly as before. Hell, even moving twenty percent faster would be better than nothing.

The pain hit him above the eye again. This time it was so bad that he'd actually dropped one of his guns and took a knee.

"See," called out Emiliano, who was demonstrating his incredible strength by using one of his zombie "shields" to point at Jin, "even your new man there has enough sense to drop his weapons and bend a knee to the superior warrior in his midst."

"You okay, chief?" Raina asked.

"Nope. Whatever they did to me during integration is making me pretty damned useless."

He was pissed. What point was there for him to be a cop if he couldn't even shoot someone? "Glug," he choked out as a white light flashed across his vision and dropped him onto his back.

This was *not* going to work.

At all.

"*Raina,*" Director Fysh said, "*go ahead and shoot the zombies behind us. Aim for their heads.*"

Jin heard the brrrrrrt sound multiple times, followed by the thumps of bodies striking the ground. It was an incredibly smart tactic that Jin wished he'd thought of before his new boss did. As it stood, though, he was barely able to think past the pain currently gripping his entire being.

"It was a valiant effort, Emiliano," Director Fysh said, "but I think we both know where this is going."

Taking a deep breath, Jin forced himself to relax. He thought of the ocean and the sandy beaches. It got him beyond the agony and into a more manageable level of pain.

"You always were quite formidable, Chief Fysh."

"It's Director Fysh now, remember?"

"Ah, yes. How forgetful of me." Emiliano's chuckle sounded like slabs of meat sloshing around in a bucket of water. "Only the Para*Ab*normal Police Department would be stupid enough to promote their best into positions where they become impotent."

Jin found it difficult to disagree with Emiliano at that point. He felt like a complete waste of space. If they made it out of this alive, he was going to have something done about it, too, even if it meant grabbing hold of someone by the throat and shoving his gun up their...

...no no no...

"Think about the ocean," he whispered to himself as he fought to stave off another round of anguish. "Think about the ocean."

"It's quite a shame you took a liking to my idiot

weakling of a son," Emiliano said, still speaking with Director Fysh. "We could have made a powerful team."

"*Raina, take out the ones to his left and right please.*"

Brrrrrt…brrrrrt.

"Hector is twice the man you'll ever be," Director Fysh stated.

"I am?" Hector sounded pretty shocked.

"Yeah," agreed Sofia, "he is?"

Director Fysh obviously ignored them both. "Your shields are all that's left, Emiliano, and we both know they're not going to hold up to my officer's gun."

Jin's head cleared just enough to glance up at the monstrous zombie. It hurt, but he forced himself to watch, just in case something even worse happened. Jin wasn't afraid of dying, but he at least wanted to see it coming.

"We shall meet another time," Emiliano said as his eyes began to glow a slightly orange color.

"Raina!"

It was too late. Her shots hit nothing but empty air.

In the time it took for her to pull the trigger, Emiliano leapt off to the right like a bolt of lightning. He had his minions in his hands, which was somewhat surprising. Jin would've assumed the zombie couldn't have given a shit about either of them.

Trying to follow the blur of their motion made Jin comprehend how people must have seen him during his assassinations.

"There and there!" Emiliano yelled, pointing at four of Hector's guards. "Pick them up and use them as shields!"

Ah, that's why he'd kept hold of the two zombies. It

allowed him the ability to bring back guards to use as reinforcements.

Zombie or not, the guy wasn't dumb.

On top of that, Jin understood Raina knew better than to fire on them at that point. It was one thing to kill off zombies who were attacking you, but it was quite another to put bullets into Hector's incapacitated guards. While nobody would doubt those poor guards were bound to be zombies themselves in a matter of time, shooting them was not something any PPD cop was going to do at that point.

"What's with all the noise out here?" said a woman who had walked out of the side building as Jin struggled to get to his feet. She stepped toward the zombies. "Emiliano? I thought you were dead."

"Carina," Emiliano said, that wicked smile of his falling into place, "I *am* dead."

She kept walking toward him, her face masked in confusion.

"Stay back, Carina!" Hector called out. "He'll—"

Too late. Emiliano launched one of Hector's guards through the air at Raina's car before jumping forward and grabbing Carina and pulling her in close.

The poor guard who had been launched landed on the hood of the car, smashing it as his head cracked the windshield.

His head got the worst of that collision.

"No!" Raina said, raising Bernadette back up to point it at Emiliano. "I loved that car, you…you…poop!"

Everyone glanced at her for a moment.

"Did you just call him a poop?" asked Rudy.

"Yes, and I'm sorry, but look what he did to my poor car!"

She'd totally missed the point of Rudy's comment.

"I'll be coming for you soon, boy," Emiliano said, ignoring Raina's outrage. "Once you're in my army, you'll *truly* be a man, no matter what Director Fysh says. Sofia, I'll be back to fetch you, Cano, and Alejandro as well." He didn't wait for a response. "As for you wimpy little PPD cops, you'll be going to the Vortex before the end of the week, so you might want to get your affairs in order."

Once he'd said his piece, he turned and jumped the fence with the other zombies and their human luggage, before disappearing over the hill.

CHAPTER 28

Vestin

*V*estin maintained a stern stare at Emiliano. The man had lost several members of the army. While Vestin cared very little about the deaths themselves, he *did* care about losing numbers. The math was simple: the more zombies he had under his control, the more territory he would be able to dominate.

"I recognize that you brought back replacements, Emiliano," he was saying, "but had you kept your temperament under control, we would have not only the original soldiers but also many more added."

"Yes…my lord."

"Uppercase, Emiliano."

The zombie groaned. "Yes, My Lord."

"Good."

He wanted to turn the screws royally, but he refrained. A man like Emiliano was fragile, even if he would never admit it. His ego was one that needed incessant stroking. The moment he felt undervalued, he would cause all sorts of havoc.

That didn't mean Vestin was worried the zombie would ever attack him personally. It simply wasn't possible. Well, technically, it *was* but it would require a level of magic that superseded his own, and Vestin knew well that nothing out there existed to even match what he'd developed. As it stood, Vestin had cornered the market and he wasn't about to share his secrets, nor would he create franchises. Every area that his army took over would have generals, of course, but they would have only enough power to make basic decisions. All top-level determinations would be made by Vestin and *only* Vestin.

"Lesson learned," he said to Emiliano, offering him a satisfied smile, "and now we move on. The replacements will be effective, I'm sure."

"Actually, I have brought back one who may prove very useful, My Lord."

It was nice to see Emiliano's resilience. Prior to him becoming a zombie, Vestin would have assumed the ability to change on a dime like that would not have been possible, or at least not probable. Yet further proof that *Shaded Past #13* was rather impressive.

"Someone who is good with cooking, possibly?" Vestin asked, leaning back in his chair. "Maybe a mechanic?"

If Vestin were to hazard a guess, he would've said that Emiliano was furrowing his brow. It was difficult to tell with his flesh in a never ending state of shedding.

"No, it's a witch."

Vestin sat back up. "A witch?"

"Bring her in!" Emiliano called out, causing a couple of zombies to usher a woman into the room. "This is Carina. She was my witch for a long time. Now, she's yours, My Lord."

Carina gave Emiliano a shocked look.

Vestin approved of that. Seeing that her previous boss was now the subject of another was perfect. It demonstrated he was now not only Emiliano's superior, but hers as well.

"Are you a Dark Witch?" he asked hopefully.

"No."

"My Lord," Emiliano whispered, correcting her. "Lord Vestin's weird about that."

"He's not *my* lord." She gave Emiliano a once over. "Neither are you, anymore."

Vestin grinned, accepting that maybe she hadn't understood her new place in the chain of command, after all. "She's correct, Emiliano, at least for the moment. You are under my spell; she is not. In due time she'll have her place."

"Not if you expect me to do magic for you," Carina replied, nonplussed.

"Oh, you'll do precisely as I say when I have you under my—"

"Spell," she finished for him. "Yes, I understand how it all works, and it's clear you understand that only witches and warlocks can fall under the venom of a vampire's bite. Well, and some slugs, I suppose."

"Yes, about that limitation, you should know that—"

"The problem, Lord Vasectomy…" she pushed forward.

He frowned, "It's Vestin."

"...is that you can't put a witch under your venom and expect them to be able to tap into their normal reserves." She shook her head in disappointment. "All educated people know that."

Vestin searched his memories, not certain if she was accurate or not. Then again, she was a witch and he wasn't one. For him to make judgment calls about her gifts would be equivalent to her making judgments about his. Neither of them could stand in each other's shoes, so neither of them were qualified to make such assessments.

It was just that he'd never heard such a thing mentioned in all of his readings as a boy. To be fair, it wasn't as though vampire schools paid too much attention to anyone who wasn't a vampire. Everything they taught about other races, classes, and professions that weren't deemed important to The Vampirium (the governing board of schools for vampires) was peripheral at best.

Fortunately, he was an excellent judge of character and he could nearly always spot someone who was speaking untruths.

Looking directly into her eyes, he posed the question in a very direct way. "You are telling the truth about my venom impeding your ability to do magic?"

Her eyes remained locked on his. "As far as you know."

"Hmmm."

"Got you there, boss...erm, My Lord." Emiliano went to clear his throat, which resulted in a hunk of esophagus shooting across the room to stick against the wall. "Sorry, My Lord."

Vestin sighed.

Why were things always such a chore?

It was time to turn his attention away from the witch for now. There was another pressing issue, and it was one Emiliano was hopefully capable of resolving, unless he was prone to repeating mistakes. If so, Vestin would find a replacement for him, though he so despised that process.

"I'm assuming you were incapable of dispatching the Paranormal Police Department's officers?"

"Why would you assume that?" Emiliano asked, looking worried.

"Simple, Emiliano," Vestin replied, steepling his fingers. "You lost a number of my soldiers, remember, which would certainly mean that it happened while you were in the process of eliminating the police, right?"

"Oh, uh…" Emiliano slumped slightly.

Vestin sorely wanted to rub it in, but he had to remember yet again who he was dealing with. The poor zombie needed his ego intact in order to thrive. It was unfortunate, proving once more that management carried with it a weight in curses.

"These things happen, Emiliano…once." He wanted to stand and pace, but he decided it was more powerful for him to remain seated and calm. "I would imagine a man of your cunning ability would know what to do now, however, yes?"

"Um…yesssss?"

It was all Vestin could do to not grin. "Yes, yes, I'm sure you recognize that going *back* to your old house with your new soldiers at the moment would be apropos since it would absolutely provide you with the optimal time to strike." Emiliano's eyes were darting about. Sigh. "And, I shall save you from having to explain to me the reason it's optimal."

"Thanks."

"It's because you are fully aware the PPD would have left the area by now, your son would not even entertain the idea that you'd be back anytime soon, and the guards you were unable to bring with you before will very likely still be dazed from your earlier attack."

Emiliano was nodding. "Uh…yeah. I was thinking all that, My Lord."

Unfortunately, the oaf continued to stand there, clearly baffled by what steps he should take next.

"I shouldn't wish to delay your work, then, Emiliano."

"Hmmm?" Emiliano looked around again. "Oh, yeah, right. I'll…uh…I'll go put…uh…my plan in action, My Lord."

Carina pinched the bridge of her nose and bent her head forward as Emiliano left the area. It seemed not only Vestin considered the man to have the wit of a damp stone.

"A bit of a dullard, that one," Vestin said.

"And it's apparently grown worse with his zombieism."

"Indeed." Vestin rocked slightly in his chair as he continued gazing at his newfound prize. "A witch could be quite a boon to my army, you know?"

"I can't see how," she replied, defiant. "I don't use dark energy."

"Oh, come now." Vestin knew how this would end, or at least he knew the two ways it could potentially end. "I'm well aware that you *could* use dark energy, should you so choose, as you have spent much time doing that very thing for Emiliano."

"Yes, but that time of my life has come to an end and I'll be damned if I'll do it again for yet another vile boss."

"Hmmm." Vestin surveyed her for a moment, allowing the heat of her disposition to fester some. "Do note I've decided I shall not bite you for the moment, at least not until I've had your claim about it interfering with your ability to do magic verified." He breathed in through his nose. "That doesn't mean I won't outright kill you for not doing what I command you to do, however, and I shall be sure the process is as drawn out and uncomfortable as possible."

In that moment, Carina's disposition shifted.

"Kill me?"

"Quite literally, yes. Your existence on this plane of reality shall cease."

"Uncomfortably?"

"Insidiously so, mmm-hmmm."

"I see." She swallowed hard. "So, I'm going to be doing dark magic then?"

Vestin replied with a patronizing smile, saying, "I believe that's what we're agreeing upon, yes."

Her demeanor shifted yet again. If nothing else, she was rather a chameleon. "Sounds swell. I mean, it's not like I haven't been doing this already for quite some time, as you've said…Lord Vaginitis."

"It's Vestin, and I'd suggest you commit that to memory as my patience for such things is limited."

That's when Prender rushed into the room, grinning from ear to ear. He gave Carina a once-over, a quick nod, and then placed a box on Vestin's desk. He tapped on it and said, "They've arrived, My Lord!"

"I can see that Prender, yes." He quickly motioned between Prender and the witch. "Prender, this is our new witch, Carina; Carina, this is my second-in-command, Prender."

They shared their hellos as Vestin opened the box and took out a few of the flyers. They were the same as the original mockup he'd seen for *Shaded Past #13*, only these were on heavier stock.

He had to admit they made his "business" look rather respectable.

He handed one to Carina. "This is what we'll be pushing."

"Another fancy drug?" she replied. "I've seen so many of these that I—"

"Oh, it's not a drug," Vestin interrupted. "It's a way of life." He flicked his hand. "Or possibly death, depending on how you look at it."

Her eyes snapped up to his a moment later. "Wait, this is the stuff that's causing zombieism?"

"Indeed, but not just any zombieism." He flashed his fangs. "I control them. You've seen it with Emiliano already, no?"

That only caused her eyes to open more. "But that shouldn't be possible. Vampires have never been able to dominate other supernaturals, except my kind, and you can't even do that very well."

"Times have changed, my dear Carina. I have created a way to dominate all of them, twisting them to my will." He tilted his head slightly. "In fact, it makes one wonder if

I could share my gift with you without it depleting your ability to cast the magic I shall require."

She licked her lips nervously, clearly doing her best to think of something. "If you're wrong, you'll only have another zombie on your side."

It was a valid point, assuming her earlier declaration had been true. And now that his second-in-command had arrived, he could find out.

"Prender, you're a bit of a study on witches and warlocks, no?"

He looked downright chuffed. "Oh, yes. I was top of my class in Netherworld Proper. In fact, my dissertation was on—"

"Yes, yes," Vestin shushed the man. "All thrilling, I'm sure. Anyway, the question I have is if a witch's ability would in any way be diminished should she fall under the venom of a vampire?"

"Absolutely, My Lord."

"Told ya."

Vestin pursed his lips. "Indeed, you did."

"It wasn't always like that," Prender began, going into a lecture. "It happened because of an evolutionary chain of events that—"

Putting the box top back in place, Vestin interrupted the man yet again. "I'm sure this is all rather fascinating to someone who cares. Sadly for you, I'm not that person." He waved at his second, who'd lost his chuffness. "Take these and begin distribution, assuming you have a location set?"

"Yes, My Lord," Prender replied, though it was

somewhat subdued now. "Janet Smith has helped me to garner a place down by Hippie Beach."

"Excellent. I'm assuming it's nice?"

"She said it would suffice to fit your needs, My Lord."

"I'm sure it will."

Vestin had his doubts.

CHAPTER 29

Jin

To say he was irritated would have been sorely understating how Jin felt. It'd been a shitty day from the start and to have it end with a fogged brain in a situation where he'd been unable to help the very people he was supposed to be leading was patently unacceptable.

Fortunately, Director Fysh agreed completely.

Unfortunately, it meant he'd been forced to go through yet another round of integration to undo some of the crap they'd done to him.

He'd actually been pretty impressed with how Director Fysh had handled everything. She went straight in and tore into all the people who'd pieced together Jin, Version 2.0. She'd been relentless. It'd gotten so bad, in fact, that they'd called in the Director of Integrations.

That poor bastard got the worst of it from Director Fysh.

Even though it'd all happened inside of an office with

the door closed, everyone could see the happenings through the windows.

It wasn't pretty.

Never in all his years had Jin seen a finger wave as fast as Director Fysh's. She'd been standing at the man's desk, leaning on it, and tearing into the dude like there was no tomorrow.

By the time she was done, they not only undid *some* of the crap they'd done to him, they'd undone *all* of it. He wasn't sure if they added other stuff, but his memories had been fully restored, his taste for the kill—bad people only, of course—returned, and his magic once again flowed as it had done since he'd first gotten his ink in his teens.

While it felt great to be his old self again, he struggled to accept how they'd allow him to return topside like that. He knew what he was capable of, and he knew he wouldn't do anything without definite cause, but there'd been a reason he'd gone through the initial integration in the first place. For them to wholesale turn that around was unbelievable.

"How are you feeling?" Director Fysh asked as Jin sat on the bench, slowly recovering from his second round of fun.

"Pleased that I didn't soil the plastic that time."

"We take our wins where we can get them." She crossed her legs and checked her datapad. "You're not fully back to what you were, but it's close."

"What's missing?" Jin couldn't sense anything.

"Think about killing someone."

"Huh?"

"Let's imagine a perpetrator is trying to light up a downtown city block. What would you do?"

"Shoot him." He'd said it as if it was nothing. Frankly, it was. If a person was causing harm like that to a bunch of innocents, Jin would react regardless of any badge he wore. But he felt there was more to it in his thinking at the moment. "Gotta protect the innocent, right?"

Yes, it was right. You did. Ah, maybe that was it? Maybe they'd just kept in the PPD cop duty stuff he'd received in his original integration?

"Great," she said, looking pleased. "Now, pretend some asshole cut you off at an intersection or something."

"A what?"

"Car intersection. Never mind, you're still fuzzy. It's okay. We'll go with something easier." She set the datapad down and focused on him. "Imagine you've been standing in line for two hours in order to…what do you like to do most?"

"Read."

"Really?" It pained him slightly that she was surprised by that, but he let it go. "Okay, so we'll say a new book has arrived and you're standing in line to get a copy when some jerkwad walks up and cuts in front of you. What would you do?"

"I'd probably kill the…glug!"

He fell forward, the pain flashing through his brain again.

"There it is," Director Fysh said with a satisfied smile as Jin spasmed on the floor, looking up at her. "It'll pass in about a minute or so." She picked up her datapad again. "Just think of your happy place."

He did, and fast. The ocean, the beach, the breeze, the sunset...it calmed him, taking away the pain slowly. One thing was for sure, he wasn't going to be a threat to anyone who didn't have it coming. Now, it could be argued a line-cutter *did* have it coming, but his integration deemed it too minor of an offense to warrant capital punishment.

A few minutes later, he crawled back into his chair and rasped, "I got it. I can only kill people while in the line of duty, and only if they've proven themselves in need of killing."

She patted his knee. "Well done. Not everyone is inherently bad who does bad things, but sometimes their off-days require a bit of a course correction. You're still allowed to help them reset their compasses."

"Right. But when they're bad—or in need of a compass resetting—I'm able to do what I need to do?"

"Completely, Chief Kannon," she answered, putting the datapad away and getting to her feet. "I couldn't rightly turn my precinct over to someone who flops around on the ground in the face of danger every time it rears its head, now could I?"

The shame returned. "No."

"Don't feel bad. You weren't at fault." She glanced at the office door. "I read the report and the changes they made before. You wouldn't have been able to squash a bug without having a migraine. Ridiculous." She reached out and helped him to his feet. "As it stands now, you'll be precisely what the PPD is going to need if *your* team is going to manage the new zombie threat."

"Good," he said, feeling somewhat better to know that

at least his boss was on his side. He couldn't say how his new crew felt about everything yet, but he had the feeling he'd find out soon enough. "I'm much more effective than that, so you know."

She patted the side of her briefcase. "I'm fully aware, Chief Kannon. It's a rarity for someone to get to one thousand kills, especially in your previous vocation."

If nothing else, he had that accolade on his side. No, it wasn't an award for solving world hunger or a plaque given to someone for helping to arrange a much-needed peace treaty, but for his new position in the PPD having one thousand confirmed kills was almost as important as it was for his old position in the Assassins Guild.

It might take some fieldwork in his new role as the chief to prove his worth to his subordinates, but they'd soon see his skills on full display, especially if there were zombies involved. Not even an M134 Minigun could keep pace with Jin Kannon's speed when he was fully engaged.

"May I offer you a word of advice?" Director Fysh said as they walked toward the transporter.

"Please."

"Be who you are, Chief Kannon. Don't try to sugarcoat it or hide it. Don't try to get on everyone's good side. You'll do fine." She stepped into the booth. "Again, I've read your records. You weren't only effective, your peers respected you for who you were. You walk your talk. The files show that. Continue doing so and your team will follow you every step of the way, assuming you're not a dick about it."

"Right."

CHAPTER 30

Hector

Once the PPD left, Hector worked with Sofia, Cano, and Alejandro to pick up the guards who hadn't been taken by the zombies.

Hector's brain was cramping at the memory of seeing his father in zombie form. In some respects, it was truly how he'd always seen the man, even if only from an emotional point of view. Emiliano had always been a vile beast; the zombieism merely served to unveil the physical manifestation of the true man.

"What happened, boss?" asked one of his guards who was still pretty groggy from being clobbered. "I thought I saw zombies and then…I don't remember anything."

"Let's just get you inside so the doctor can check you over."

The guy's eyes cleared immediately and he sprung to his feet, looking as though he'd just awoken from a refreshing nap.

"Actually, I suddenly feel great! No need to see the doc for me!"

"We have to see the doc?" said another guard, who also suddenly got a spring in her step. "Why bother? He's probably busy. Lots of…uh…things to poke around with, I mean."

Ah, right.

"Calm down, everyone," Hector called out. "I'm not sending you to the doctor as werewolves. I just want him to check each of you over to make sure there are no dire injuries."

"But, boss," the guard next to him said with a look of worry, "Dr. Sanchez is *very* thorough. *Very*."

Hector wasn't going to argue that. If he were being honest, he wouldn't want to see the doctor either, even if he'd just been knocked out by a zombie.

But his responsibility was to make sure his guards were in top shape, no matter what.

"I'll have a quick discussion with him to make sure he doesn't do his *normal* inspections, okay?"

They all relaxed immediately.

Too bad everything was interrupted by the sound of gurgling.

"Shit!" yelled Cano, pointing off to the field on their left. "They're back!"

Then, like a team of secret service agents, Sofia, Cano, and—surprisingly—Alejandro grabbed Hector and lifted him clear off his feet. They rushed him up the stairs and into the house before he had a chance to utter a single word. He wouldn't have known what to say anyway, other than maybe, "Everyone run!"

Instead, his faithful guards could be heard firing their weapons and then screaming.

There was a finality to their screams, too.

Hector struggled to get free. "We have to get out there and help them!"

"Help them do what, boss?" Sofia asked as they continued rushing him through the house. "Die?"

She was right, but if there was any one thing Emiliano had ingrained into Hector's skull it was that only cowards ran. At that moment, Hector felt the depth of those teachings. He was helpless to get away from the grip of the three people holding him, but that didn't matter. He still felt like a coward.

They took him down a set of stairs, through a corridor, and then into a secret passage he'd never seen before.

"What is this place?"

"An escape tunnel," Sofia said. "It'll take us out to the beach."

"I've never seen any of this before, but I'm sure my father knows all about it, right? He'll just follow us." He struggled again. "Put me down! I can walk from here. I don't need to be carried."

The three guards stopped and let him go.

Sofia gave the other guards a quick look. "Yes, Emiliano knows about the tunnels. He oversaw their construction. But there are numerous exit points, so he'll never know which one we took."

"Unless he floods all of them with zombies and they get back to him with intel," noted Cano.

"True, but by then we'll be far enough away that he

won't attempt to catch us."

Hector eyed her. "Why are we running?"

"Even I know the answer to that, boss," Alejandro said. "You can't manage a cartel if you're dead." Hector was about to argue when Alejandro held up a hand. "Look, boss, you ain't your father and you never will be. He was tough, smart, and ruthless."

"He was also better looking," added Sofia, "in a rugged kind of way."

"Gee, thanks guys. This is *exactly* the kind of motivational speech I needed right now."

Alejandro's face grew more serious than Hector could recall, except for when the man was engaged in battle, or about to be. "The point I'm trying to make, boss, is that we don't want a zombie leading *The Dogs*. We may be a lot of things, but I think we can all agree that zombies running the show would mean the community you've been thinking of building ain't ever going to happen."

Hector studied all three of them with a bit of shock.

Could it be that his words from earlier had actually resonated with them? Was it possible that these typically violence-thirsty people—aside from Cano, who had turned out to be remarkably normal—were seriously growing fond of the idea of living in a more familial space?

The looks on their faces told him all he needed to know.

They were basically emotionally scarred children who wanted nothing more than to have a place they could actually call "Home."

"Okay," he said, "I believe I understand."

He gave a quick look around, not sure which tunnel he was supposed to take. It still bugged him that he'd not even known about these hidden caverns in the first place. He wasn't surprised by it, knowing how Emiliano would've been more than happy to sacrifice Hector at the drop of a hat, but it still hurt.

"Get me to the San Diego Paranormal Police Department," he commanded.

"Wait, what?" Sofia asked.

"You heard me." He pointed at the door they'd entered through. "You brought me down here because you knew there's no way we're going to be able to fight those zombies alone. You also know that if we bring Mr. Becerra into this, he's going to send an army that will very likely fall to my father, turning them into an even larger force that we'll never be able to contain."

"Meaning we need to team up with the cops," said Cano. The other two spun their heads toward him. "The boss is right, guys." He shrugged. "I'm all about keeping the business in the family, but the family is out there being slaughtered and there's nothing we can do to save them. We may not love the cops, but they have technology we don't. They have resources we don't." It was amazing to see Cano in this light. "Most importantly, I'd rather see them lose *their* reinforcements than see us lose *ours*."

That honestly wasn't what Hector was thinking. He'd prefer that nobody be sent to the slaughterhouse, but if it was the kind of talk that got Sofia and Alejandro to act, so be it.

Slowly, Sofia began to nod.

"You're not as dumb as I thought, Cano."

"Thanks?"

She gave him a wry smile and then turned and ran into the third tunnel. "Follow me!"

CHAPTER 31

Petey

The sun was going down, which meant Petey's least favorite potheads were about to show up. They always arrived around this time. That, in and of itself, was amazing since they happened to be the most consistently baked people he'd ever met. How they were able to maintain *any* schedule at all was a study in fascination.

As expected, two people rounded the corner and started trudging their way.

"Here they come," he said to Raffy, who merely grunted in reply.

Reef and Zooie weren't bad people, but they were awkward. They were normals. That wasn't such a bad thing. It was simply strange because they didn't seem impacted by null or hidden zones in the least. They were able to walk back and forth between the normals' area and the supers' area as if there was nothing separating them.

It probably had to do with how their brains effectively ran on hops and resin.

All supers knew that drug and/or drink-induced impairment in normals allowed them to bypass the majority of supernatural blockades. It also allowed them to see supers jumping in and out of portals. These two had become the most relied-upon dealers in the area, though, meaning they were allowed in on the secrets regarding supers. Most normals were kept in the dark, but a few were actually *given* the key to the vault of secrecy. It usually happened with casino workers, hotel staff, and top-level executives at supernatural-run businesses. These two had the fogged brain *and* the key.

Zooie and Reef were the first drug dealers Petey had ever heard of being let in on the deal. There'd probably been more, of course, but only if they were as perpetually fried as these guys.

"Sup, dudes?" asked Reef.

"It's like 7:30 or something," Zooie announced as she always did, "but it's 4:20 somewhere!"

They both wore outfits that were the spitting image of Raffy's getup, including the glasses, though they currently had them pushed up to the top of their heads. They'd even allowed their hair to grow out all over their bodies.

They worshiped Raffy, considering him the "Mo-i," which meant "King" in the Hawaiian language. It sounded like they were saying "Moh-ee" whenever they addressed him that way.

"Just chillin' and soakin' in the peace, man," Raffy said before reaching back and scratching his ass.

"Truth, Mo-i," Zooie said in a stoner-chuckling way.

Reef nodded. "Inspiration, man."

Here's where they were going to go on their typical tirade about how awesome Raffy was, how he was their hero, and how they strived daily to match his level of chill…and, it seemed, stench.

It was usually too syrupy for Petey to deal with, but that was probably his pixie side speaking. Then again, it wasn't like demons were much better.

"Before you two start trying to preen his ball hairs," Petey said, "what's on the menu for today?

"I'm not preening the dude's nut forest, lopa," Reef replied, sounding slightly less than chill.

"Lopa," it turned out, was the Hawaiian word for "peasant." It'd taken Petey a while to learn that, since he didn't speak Hawaiian. The weird part was that neither did Reef or Zooie. He assumed, via some moment of inspiration that drove them to get on the Internet, or through asking a friend of theirs who may have actually been a native of Hawaii, they'd hunted for certain terms whenever needed.

Since Petey was *not* currently blitzed out of his mind, he was grumpy. Petey wasn't a complicated person. He was either pleasantly baked or irritably sober.

"First off, you both smell nearly as bad as him."

"Whoa, scro," Zooie said, smiling wide enough to show her brown teeth, "that's like the nicest thing you've ever said to us."

"Major props for sure!" agreed Reef.

"Ugh." Petey wasn't going to bother going on with his list of grievances with the two idiots. They'd totally take his words as compliments and that'd only serve to aggravate Petey even more. "Just tell me what you've got on the menu, dickheads."

Reef dug into his tattered backpack and pulled out a few bags of weed. "Your norms, yo?"

Petey nodded toward the orange bucket to his left. "Fill it up, same as every week."

"Throw in a few shrooms, man," Raffy said. "The Raffster needs to go on holiday."

It bugged Petey to no end when Raffy called himself "The Raffster," especially when he "needed to go on holiday." That meant he was going to trip balls, which ultimately led to Petey doing his best to keep his friend away from the ocean. Putting a stinkfoot in the ocean was a surefire way to kill off a lot of fish, not to mention turn coral brown. On top of that, it took a few days for the water to quit smelling like stinkfoot soup.

"Don't forget to tell them about the new stuff, Reefy," Zooie said.

"Ohhhh! Right!" Reef dug around in the bag some more and pulled out what looked like a flyer. "Check it, scros. Not any in my pack, but there's a building over yonder with hits." He stood up proud. "Make sure to tell 'em Reef and Zooie sent ya so we get our props, yo?"

Petey studied the leaflet for a few moments.

Shaded Past #13.

Sounded interesting, but a scent from the card hit him that made his sphincter tighten. With all the odors in the air, it was amazing he caught it at all.

He handed it over to Raffy.

"Take a whiff of that."

Raffy did and then turned his head toward Petey. "Vamp."

"Yep."

"*The Dogs* ain't known for vamps, man."

"Nope." Petey looked up at the two ganj-heads. "Either of you tried this stuff yet?"

"Not our bag, lopa," Reef answered. "We're all about the weed."

"And the booze," amended Zooie.

"Truth."

While he shouldn't have cared in the least, Petey kind of did. These two morons were his connection, so he felt somewhat obligated to protect them. It was either that or he'd have to find new connections, and he hated doing that. In Petey's estimation it was better to deal with the bullshit that came with consistent relationships than the horror of creating new ones.

Maybe he was an introvert? Probably more likely he was a can't-stand-people-vert. Bah! Even with their faults, Reef and Zooie seemed like a couple of decent kids.

Whenever he got a bit sentimental, he knew it was his demon side talking.

"Stay away from this shit, you hear?" he said seriously.

They backed up slightly. "Slam on the brakes, lopa."

"Yeah, man," agreed Zooie. "Temper the steam."

He wanted to throttle them both. "Look, idiots, I don't know what this stuff is, but it doesn't smell right and you need to stay away from it."

Zooie motioned toward Raffy. "He doesn't smell right and you've never given us gripes about hanging here."

"Truth."

Petey rolled his eyes and glanced over at Raffy, imploring him to say something to his "flock."

Raffy scratched his ass again and said, "Petey's right, scros. You know I'm all about tryin' new adventures, man, but...uh...as your Moleheap..."

"Mo-i," corrected Petey.

"...I, like, hereby, you know, decree, man, because of the...the...the logicalization and such of it, or whatever, that, like...uh...a big fat *no* on this stuff, man."

"But why, Mo-i?" asked Reef.

"There are...uh...many threads here, man. I mean, you have to see, like, the...uh...start or maybe the middle... uh..."

"He's trying to say because this shit is dangerous," Petey pointed out.

"Yeah, man. That."

The fact was Petey and Raffy didn't really know if it was dangerous or not, but it was a valid assumption for three reasons.

First, it had a brand name. Whenever that happened, like *Happy Product #7*, it meant people would give it a shot and get addicted really quickly.

Second, this one had 13 iterations. That was an obvious indicator it'd taken a long time to make *sure* it was going to get people addicted fast.

Third, vampires were involved, leading him to understand there was a new cartel in town. If so, they'd have to be looking to take some turf from *The Dogs*.

Nobody, especially stoners, wanted to get in the middle of a turf war.

People died doing that.

"Just promise us you'll stay away from that crap," Petey said, wishing he hadn't needed to point it out.

"If Mo-i says to bypass that particular freeway, we'll take an off-ramp," Zooie confirmed.

"Truth."

They finished up their business and walked on to whereever their next drop-off point was located. Petey didn't know and he'd never cared to find out. They were merchants to him. Nothing more.

Dammit. That wasn't true, but he was going to push himself to continue thinking that way.

It was easier.

"You, like, think we should tell the cops or something, man?" Raffy asked, sounding almost coherent while reading the flyer again.

Though it was against his better judgment, Petey said, "Probably."

CHAPTER 32

Jin

W hen they returned to the PPD headquarters in San Diego, Jin Kannon felt great. The fuzziness had disappeared, his magic flowed freely, though his PPD tattoo tingled a bit whenever he tapped into the well of power to test things, and his confidence had returned.

He felt whole again.

As soon as he and Director Fysh walked through the front door, however, they were greeted with a scene that consisted of a bunch of guards holding members of *The Dogs* at gunpoint. There was also a huge, extremely hairy guy wearing a beach outfit, and he was holding a garden gnome.

The smell in the room was enough to knock over a rhino.

"Director Fysh!" Guard Levi Snoodle barked. "Chief Kannon!" All the guards quickly saluted before putting their hands back on their weapons. "We've been detaining these people, sirs. Uh…ma'am and sir."

Director Fysh gave an almost imperceptible shake of her head.

"These guards will drive you batty if you're not careful, Chief Kannon."

He allowed himself a small grin. *"I've already been through here once, Director. I'm well aware of their desire to impress."*

"Quite." She paused. *"I'm not really surprised to see Hector and his people, but Raffy and Petey seem out of place."*

Jin could neither agree or disagree with that assessment, since he had no clue who the other two were.

"Excellent work, guards," Director Fysh said. "We'll take it from here." She walked forward, waving at the guards to lower their weapons and for everyone else to join her in the elevator. At the last moment, though, she held out a hand, blocking who Jin believed to be Raffy from joining. "It may be best if you two took the stairs. We'd like to make it upstairs without passing out first." She leaned her head out. "Let the stinkfoot and the gnome use the stairwell, Snoodle."

"Yes, ma'am, sir!"

The stinkfoot didn't seem bothered. He simply turned and headed toward the stairs.

Once the doors closed, Sofia said, "Why are there two stoners here, Director Fysh? I sure would hate to learn those fuckers are informants."

"Then don't learn it, Sofia." Her look was deadly serious. So much so that Sofia averted her gaze. That was impressive. "They're under our protection. If anything happens to either of them, aside from a much-needed shower or ten, I'll bring the power of the force down on your heads so fast you'll wish you'd been slaughtered by those zombies today."

Hector moved to speak next. "There's no need for threats, Frannie...Director Fysh. We have a common issue right now with the very zombies you speak of. They came back after you left."

"Oh?"

"Yes, and our community needs us to think beyond ourselves at the moment." He looked at his minions carefully. "Therefore, our memories regarding *anything* that occurs during our need to work together will be short."

Everyone nodded.

Jin found that somewhat heartening.

The doors opened and they all poured out, walking to the main area. All the officers were waiting, including Miss Kane.

"Glad you're back, Chief Kannon," said Raina. "You, too, Director Fysh. I just meant because he—"

"It's okay, Raina," Director Fysh interrupted. "Everyone relax. Things are about to get dicey around here, and I mean that in a way that's worse than typical."

Raffy and the gnome walked in next.

"Raffy?" said Chimi. "Petey?"

"Shall I turn on the sprinkler system, Director Fysh?" asked Rusty through the speakers. "There seems to be some kind of foreign contaminant in the air."

"It's just a stinkfoot, Rusty," Chimi answered before the Director could. "A very sexy and—"

"Ye might wanna get after sprayin' some potpourri type somethin' or other in here, and fast! Otherwise, our resident cyclops is gonna make a scene."

The air suddenly changed from the smell of pot and rot to something altogether different. It wasn't pleasant, but it wasn't horrible either. Actually, that's not accurate. It was both pleasant *and* horrible.

Lacey waved her wand over her nose. "Egads! Smells like someone shat a Christmas tree, it does!"

"Deal with it," Director Fysh said. "We have work to do." She then stepped back and motioned at Jin. "It's your show now, Chief Kannon. What's the plan?"

Jin wasn't sure what to say. His frame of reference was typically one that provided him with a sheet of paper containing a name and photograph. Sometimes there was even a location, but usually not. He was still green in his role here, however. He knew almost nothing about the area, and he'd only scratched the surface in learning about his new team.

In other words, he was *not* the most qualified person to lead this charge.

Too bad life never seemed to gift wrap solutions for the problems it launched at you.

That only solidified his thoughts further.

Jin quickly jumped to the connector. *"Maybe you should retain control until this is over, Director Fysh? I don't mind stepping aside and acting in a supporting role."*

"It's appreciated, Chief Kannon," she replied. *"I will be supporting you and the crew during this fiasco, but I'll be more effective in my new role than in the field. Besides, I've always*

been a firm believer that trials by fire pull the best out of people. And this, Chief Kannon, is a scorcher."

No shit.

He let out a quick breath and addressed the crew.

"Thank you, Director Fysh." He took off his hat. "The first thing I'd like to do is apologize for my inability to be of much help earlier when we were attacked by the zombies."

"Zombies?" blurted the gnome. "Shit." He looked up at his stinky pal. "That's what the stupid *Shaded Past #13* is doing. But why zombies?"

"Sorry, what are you talking about?"

Raffy lowered his sunglasses slightly. "You're, like, uh, the new chief now?"

"Yes. My name is Jin Kannon."

"Cool name, man." Raffy then sat the talking gnome on Raina's desk. "Well, it's like this, right? We were like…you know…doing our thing and such, man. It's a lot of work and all but we make it go, dig? So like…"

"He's trying to say that we were given a flyer for some new drug and it was tainted with the scent of a vampire."

Hector's head shot up. "What?"

"I'll kill the fuckers!" Sofia said. "Nobody muscles in on our turf."

The physical changes in Hector's guards told Jin they all agreed with that sentiment.

"Might want to take control of this, Chief Kannon," Director Fysh said.

He gave her a nod.

"Good!" They all spun and looked at him as if he was nuts. "I don't mean that it's good about the drug. I mean it's good that we have a lead. It's also apparent we have a common purpose, though I'm not sure why a gnome and a stinkfoot would want anything to do with it."

"They're informants, chief," said Raina.

That wasn't Jin's point, but it didn't matter anyway. They were here now and that meant they were part of the team, until they weren't. That was true for everyone, he supposed.

He reached out for his hat, but decided to leave it where it was. There was comfort in having it on his head, though maybe it was more of a crutch. Either way, he left it where it was and continued on.

"It's clear nobody knows where this zombie threat is coming from, though maybe this *Shaded Past #13* stuff is a clue. Everyone who got attacked today was obviously shocked and surprised at what we saw." They were all nodding their heads. "For now we'll work to gather any information we can." He focused on Hector. "I'm assuming you're here because you've either lost control of your house completely or you're looking for some kind of assistance in keeping what you've managed to retain."

"Honestly, Chief Kannon, I believe we may currently be all that's left of *The Dogs*."

"We don't know that, Hector," Sofia challenged. "There are multiple houses and—"

"And my father knows all their weak points," Hector interrupted. "Sorry, but you know it's true. He knows them better than any of us." He put a hand on her shoulder. "But, yes, we should do what we can to see if we can salvage anyone from them." He looked back at Jin. "We just can't do that with only four people."

Jin nodded. It was strange that the PPD would stick its neck out to help the cartel, though.

"Why would we help them again, Director? I mean, if we let them suffocate, we no longer have a drug problem to contend with in the area, right?"

"Until the next enterprise jumps in to take their place, Chief Kannon. Better the devil you know..."

Fair point.

"Anyway," he went on, speaking aloud again, "I have to say that this has probably been the most interesting day I've had in twenty years." He peered over at Raina. "Please tell me this isn't normal."

"It's not. I mean, we're always dealing with one emergency or another, but this one is pretty crazy!"

That was something to hang his hat on, at least. If they got through this, things would potentially calm down. After one thousand confirmed kills, Jin Kannon was in desperate need of at least *some* calmness.

Not today. Soon, maybe, but not today.

"All right," he said, clapping his hands together as he realized the best first step would be to do the same things he did when preparing to take out a target. "We've got a lot of planning to do and a fair amount of recon work." He pointed around at the non-PPD staff. "If you're going to work with us, we'll have to agree to a chain of command where the PPD holds point. Any arguments?"

They shook their heads.

"Good."

Jin glanced out at the already-darkened sky, reminding him his first day in San Diego had not afforded him the sunset he'd hoped to see.

There was always tomorrow.

Hopefully.

"Let's get moving, people," he commanded, snatching up his hat before heading into his new office. "We've got zombies to catch!"

As everyone dispersed, he waved Raina in with him.

"Is there a beach within walking distance of here?"

"Yeah, chief," she started, but he moved his hand in a way that made clear he wanted her to keep it down. "Sorry. *Could just use the connector.*"

"*Right. I'll get used to that eventually. I just need a few minutes by myself, preferably at the beach. I have to recenter.*"

"*I totally get it. If you head out the front door of the building and go straight across the road for about two blocks, you'll hit the beach. It's not a huge stretch of sand, but it's nice enough.*"

"*Thanks, Raina. Keep everything flowing here, please? I'll be back shortly. Just need a few minutes.*"

"*No problem!*"

CHAPTER 33

Jin

Thankfully, it'd only been about a ten minute walk. The night was breezy and warm, but not too warm. The air flowing in from the ocean was nice. Having lived in the Badlands all of his life, this was almost cold in comparison to what he was used to.

Jin swung his head around to make sure nobody was nearby. Channeling his magic, he reached out for a deeper check to make sure there were no heartbeats within range.

It was clear.

Then he started talking to himself.

He'd been doing that more and more, so he figured maybe it was a subconscious way of dealing with everything that was happening to him. Was he playing the role of his own shrink? It was possible. Ever since he'd decided to focus inwardly, after completing a couple hundred assassinations, Jin had found a measure of peace.

Why he began speaking aloud was unexplained, however. He would've have blamed it on the PPD connector device, fearing his thoughts would be overheard, except he'd started doing it prior to the tattoo being added.

Ah, wait.

He no longer had the ear of Chancellor Frey.

Jin wasn't exactly someone who spoke with a lot of people, but whenever he had deeper issues to contend with, he *did* speak with Frey. In fact, it was a requirement of his job. If she deemed Jin—or any assassin—needed additional assistance beyond what she could provide, she'd set up a meeting and get them help. Jin had never required any outside psychiatry, but that was only because the Chancellor had been pretty solid at guiding him when needed.

She was out of the picture now, though, meaning he had to either find some professional help or he had to help himself.

At the moment, he chose self-help.

"Okay, Jin, let's talk this out." It felt strange, but he rolled with it. "You took this job because you wanted to be topside, at the beach."

The crashing of the waves told him he'd made the right choice about wanting to be near the ocean, if nothing else.

"The problem, buddy, is that this life is already more hectic than anything you've put yourself through in the last fifteen years."

And it was true. Early on, he'd taken a lot of crazy contracts that pushed his adrenaline. After a while, though, he'd eased off the pedal and found a pace that allowed him weeks of doing nothing but reading and relaxing.

He'd still workout and practice tactics, but that was different.

"It's day one, pal. *Day one*." He shook his head. "I know they've all said this isn't the norm, and we've got no reason to think it is, but even if it's half this crazy on any given day that'd still be *a lot* of crazy."

A gust of wind rushed across the beach, lifting the sand up to patter the side of his face. His initial reaction was to lift his arm in protection, but he didn't. Instead, he closed his eyes and felt the grains hit his right cheek. The wind hadn't been so powerful as to make it hurt. It was just a bit of tingling.

It felt kind of good, lifting his spirits...until the memories of the day flooded back in.

"Ugh. What are you going to do, Jin?" He allowed his normal senses to fully engage the surroundings. "You wanted to be in *this* situation, not the PPD one. The beach, the water, the breeze, the sunset—ah, the sunset—which you *didn't* even get a chance to witness because you were too busy playing cops and zombies." He groaned. "What are you doing, dude?"

"It's a good question," came a voice that made him grab both guns and spin around, jumping to his feet in one smooth motion.

It was Miss Kane and she was grinning at him as he quickly lowered his revolvers.

"That's a good way to die, Miss Kane," he grumbled, putting the weapons back in their holsters.

"I don't know if it'd be a *good* way, Chief Kannon, but I

could imagine worse, depending on where the bullets had landed, obviously."

He sniffed and said, "Was there something you needed?"

She glanced past him and sat down in the sand. "I come here for a bit of rest and relaxation before heading out for the night. It's something of a ritual for me. I wasn't aware you'd be here."

"Oh, sorry. I didn't know. I was just—"

"Contemplating your decision to join the force," she interrupted. "Yes, I know. It's one of the reasons I've been out here night after night for many years."

"Ah."

He sat down again, not sure what to say.

"It does get easier," she said, picking up a handful of sand before letting it slip through her fingers in a slow cascading fall. "Or maybe I've just gotten used to it. My life in the tech room *is* a bit less hectic, but it's also quite confining."

Jin nodded. "I can imagine."

"So why'd you choose to go for the position in the first place?"

"Honestly, it was the only ticket I could see to get topside." He rubbed the sand away from his cheek. "There aren't a lot of options for an assassin with my history, you know?"

That wasn't exactly true. It seemed he could've done most anything, but it was the option presented in the heat of the moment and it gave him the ability to get topside.

"Not a great reason, but it's at least an understandable one." Pulling her knees up to her chest, she added, "My situation wasn't much better. I was given a choice to work for the PPD or to spend a few years in a six-by-four cell." She rocked a little. "Getting caught hacking isn't as much fun as doing the hacking, I must say. Anyway, that was many years ago and I ended up falling in love with my work. Not the job so much, but I do love tech."

"Never been much into it myself. It's always baffled me."

"We all have our thing." They enjoyed the waves together for a few moments. "You know, you may find you actually like being the chief here. It might take some time, but if someone like me can come around, why can't someone like you?"

It was possible, certainly. He'd actually enjoyed being an assassin, after he'd gained a stronger perspective that centered around something other than vengeance. It took a long time, but he eventually got there.

This was different.

Right?

"I don't know. The crew seems nice. Odd, but nice. And now that I've gotten my brain back together from what they did to me originally in integration, I'm feeling capable of actually contributing." He took off his hat and patted the sand with it. "I just don't think I want to fight anymore." He motioned at the ocean. "I want *this*. Peace, nature…all of it."

"I hear you. Believe me, I hear you."

He gave her a look. "You want that, too?"

"Sure. Who doesn't?" She turned her face toward the moon. "There are certain expectations when you're a succubus, but I lost the fervor for playing that role a long time ago. I *do* still play it because it's what I know. It's just not truly me anymore." She laughed in a depressed way. "It probably sounds cliche, but I'd love a normal relationship with someone who gets me, treats me nicely, and maybe gives me a nice spanking now and then."

Jin gulped.

"Right…um…sounds normal, I guess."

Miss Kane turned her head back toward him. "I'm not vanilla, Chief Kannon. That'll never change. It doesn't mean that I don't want some semblance of normal, though."

"Then why keep playing the role?"

She shrugged. "Again, expectations. What else would I do? Who am I going to find who could ever possibly see beyond the fact that I'm a succubus and instead treat me like a normal person?"

Jin could do it, but he was built that way. Of course he was just as struck by her allure as anyone else. He would've had to have been a eunuch to feel otherwise. But he *could* learn to enjoy many aspects of a person. That wasn't to say he was interested in doing so, however. Or maybe he was? It was kind of early on to say. And even if he *was* interested, that didn't mean Miss Kane would feel the same about him.

Still, he could at least understand where she was coming from.

"I'm sorry it's so difficult," he said finally. "I get it, though. Just because I've spent my entire life as an assassin, everyone freaks out when I'm nearby, like I'm some blood-starved killer who can't wait to take another life." He picked up his hat and shook it off before running his thumb around its rim. "I'm not that guy. I was good at my job, that's all, and I only did it to people who were bad. Like, seriously bad."

They sat in silence for a few minutes after that, letting the sound of the waves soothe their minds.

"So what are you going to do, Chief Kannon?"

With that, he pushed himself back to his feet and offered his hand to Miss Kane. She took it and he pulled her up.

"As to that, Miss Kane, only time will tell. For now, I have to get back." He looked over his shoulder at the city. "There's a zombie problem and I've apparently gotten myself into a position that makes me responsible for fixing it."

∾

THE END

∾

Thanks for Reading

If you enjoyed this book, would you **please leave a review** at the site you purchased it from? It doesn't have to be a book report… just a line or two would be fantastic and it would really help me out!

John P. Logsdon
www.JohnPLogsdon.com

John was raised in the MD/VA/DC area. Growing up, John had a steady interest in writing stories, playing music, and tinkering with computers. He spent over 20 years working in the video games industry where he acted as designer, programmer, and producer on many online games. He's now a full-time comedy author focusing on urban fantasy, science fiction, fantasy, Arthurian, and GameLit. His books are racy, crazy, contain adult themes and language, are filled with innuendo, and are loaded with snark. His motto is that he writes stories for mature adults who harbor seriously immature thoughts.

Jenn Mitchell

Jenn Mitchell writes humorous Urban Fantasy from the heart of South Central Pennsylvania's Amish Country. When she's not writing, she enjoys traveling, crafting, cooking, hoarding cookbooks, and spending time with the World's most patient and loving significant other. She also writes Cozy Mysteries as J Lee Mitchell.

CRIMSON MYTH PRESS

Crimson Myth Press offers more books by this author as well as books from a few other hand-picked authors. From science fiction & fantasy to adventure & mystery, we bring the best stories around!

www.CrimsonMyth.com

Made in the USA
Columbia, SC
07 September 2024

41930283R00162